C000157375

That Old House:

The Bathroom

Part 2

Copyright © 2023 by Voices From the Mausoleum

All stories copyright © their respective authors. All rights reserved.

No portion of this book may be reproduced or distributed in any form or by any means, electronic or otherwise, without written permission from the publisher or author. This book is a work of fiction. Any references to historical events, real people, or real places are used fictitiously. Other names, characters, places, and events are products of the author's imagination, and any resemblance to actual events or places or persons, living or dead, is entirely coincidental.

Cover art copyright © 2023 Angel Krause (Voices From the Mausoleum)

Contents

Trigger Warning

Some stories may contain scenes of self-harm, violence, child abuse, sexual abuse, and other nefarious themes that might be triggering to some audiences.

The Rest Stop

A.L. Davidson

You should have kept going.

Sure, the drive had been long, your legs had grown weary, and your bladder was more than full, but stopping wasn't the smartest decision. The next town was only twenty miles away. Yes, it was late, but even the most remote places have their late-shift gas stations. It would have been worth the final push.

The drive was beautiful; you were in good spirits. Long drives for work were a commonality in your life, but the scenery on this route caused you to hesitate more so than normal, to delay your arrival a few moments more without a hint of remorse. You stopped so many times to snap photos, to gaze at the slopes and hues of green, to let yourself be a tourist for once. It cost you valuable time.

True, there's a reason they write songs and poetry about this place. The Shenandoah Valley is sprawling. The highways curve and stretch like a peaceful rollercoaster through the wilderness. You've managed to get through ten hours of drive time. Only two hours more until you arrive at your destination, Washington D.C. You've been waiting anxiously for a long weekend of visiting family, walking through the monuments, simply existing. You haven't simply *existed* in a long time, and the prospect of it excites you.

Well, it did. Now you're hungry and upset and a bit on edge. Rest stops were never your favorite place to be, especially on long trips. Your parents always told you they were unsafe, to never stay longer than you needed to, and never visit one at night. Especially if the lot was empty. Rest stops are ominous; it's simply the nature of urban legends and wandering minds, of barren blacktops and tree-lined roadways.

The facilities have gotten worse since the world closed down in 2020. The vending machines are, more often than not, gated and locked. Those that aren't, are rarely stocked. The coffee dispensers are always empty, the offices vacated, restrooms grody, and brochures sit tearing at the corners with faded images that no one really stops to pay attention to. They feel desolate in a dystopian-horror film sort of way. In a manner that would make the likes of Cormac McArthy and Robert Kirkman green with envy at how cruel and twisted it felt.

This far into a trip like this, in a location like this, there are few friendly places to stop. The gas stations are sketchy or closed this late at night. Even the majority of long-standing 24/7 restaurants shuttered their doors once the sun went down nowadays. You really need to stretch your legs, though. Your foot keeps falling asleep from being glued to the gas pedal. This is the last rest stop for an ungodly amount of miles, the nearest town didn't seem safe, and you needed the break.

What would five minutes hurt?

It's spooky, unsettling in the darkness, but the relief your body feels from stepping outside of your vehicle forces the doubt to retreat back into your grey matter like an unwanted thought, shoved away to keep you from dwelling on unwelcome, intrusive musings. The hours of true crime podcasts you indulged in do little to help sway the unease you feel. Normally, you'd welcome the spine-tingling unease. It feels wrong tonight.

The autumnal air is like a balm on your itchy, AC-blasted skin. You take a moment to stretch your legs on the uncomfortable bench beneath you and sip your lukewarm soda. The near-melted ice cubes hit the sides of the foam cup as you push through the flat beverage's unsatisfying flavor. The pull of caffeine is too strong.

The only other vehicle you could see upon your arrival, aside from your own, is a semi-truck that looks to be carrying produce, parked off on the other side of the lot reserved for larger vehicles. Everything is eerily quiet; even the forest seems to be muted this late into the night.

You watch a moth fly in circles, smacking into the large white streetlights above in a rhythmic pattern. You turn your eyes up to the starry skies, visible beneath the heavy foliage of oak leaves. The sky is so clear here, you wish you could stay longer.

But alas, you need to keep moving. Always be moving. A quick restroom break and you'll be back on the road. That's the plan.

Plans rarely go accordingly, though.

You notice the red sprawling letters that read '*out of order*' on the vending machine. You sure as hell won't be using the rusty looking water fountain in between the bathrooms to refill your tumbler. The massive spiderweb beneath it causes you to pause long enough to put the thought out of your mind. Somehow, a brown recluse bite seems scarier than the setting.

Your body tenses, snapping you out of your rumination as the sound of a twig snapping breaks through the silence. With careful pacing, you turn your eyes toward the noise. Your breath halts in your throat. The shadowy figure across the parking lot had not been there mere moments before. You wonder where they came from.

You take note that no new cars have arrived, and no headlights have appeared on the swerving entrance road. For a brief moment, you pause and question if it was the driver of the semi-truck down the way coming to use the facilities.

You wave a bit out of habit and Midwestern courtesy and turn to your phone. It's well after midnight. The text you sent to your cousin is still listed as undeliverable; the service is too spotty.

When you lift your eyes back up, you gasp.

The figure now stands by your car. How did you not hear him? There's no logical, no possible way he could move that fast. His presence feels unnatural. His features look fabricated, warped and thick as if someone took melted plastic and tried to work it back into something resembling a human. The grin is lopsided, lifeless, and wide.

He takes a large, quick step forward and charges at you.

You quickly head into the bathroom, into the furthest stall.

That's your biggest mistake.

As you turn to close the door, you see him approach through the open doorway. Unnaturally tall, he has to duck to fit in the frame. His frame bends at the waist like a felled tree, and contorts to allow his strange build to slink into the bathroom. He's horrifying. Dressed entirely in black. Moving with intent. You shut the door and clamor up onto the yellowed porcelain.

Don't. Move.

You don't move. You can't move.

He stomps toward you, faces the door, and there he stays.

You sit atop the toilet, knees pulled up to your chest and eyes filled with fear. Boots, mud-caked and large, place themselves under the crack of the stall door and don't move an inch. To be *that* close, that invasive, he must be pressed up against the metal. Waiting. He knows he has you trapped.

No one is coming. Not this late into the evening. Your phone shows no signal, a noticeable lack of headlights clipping through the frosted windows high above you showcases a still empty parking lot. There's no way out of this situation. You frantically send dozens of text messages, your location, reach out on all of your socials, and pray someone will answer. Your phone battery is close to dying, draining quickly and warm to the touch from its processor being overworked.

You check the screen for the fourth time in the last twenty seconds; nothing has come through. It doesn't make any sense. How could he have snuck up on you? You can't figure out how he did it. You rack your brain and still it makes no sense.

As you lift your eyes, you feel your heart thump angrily against your chest. His eyes. They peer at you through the slits. They're yellow. Motionless and sunken into his frame as if someone placed their thumbs against them and pushed them deep into his skull. His gruesome grin is shocking. Damn these American-built toilet stalls and their horrid gaps. How long has he been watching? How long did you not notice?

A deep, reverberating chuckle echoes in the high-ceilinged bathroom. The windows seemed to rattle with anger at the sound. The overhead bulbs rumble, flicker.

The stall door shakes. His head slams against the metal plating. *Clang! Clang! Clang!* You jump at every noise. The flimsy metal rod that acts as a lock won't hold, not for long. You have no idea what he wants. You only know it can't be good. The cacophony of horrendous sounds scream around you like gunfire.

Gnashing, his gnarled, angry teeth gnaw at the metal door, up and down as if it were a cob of corn, making horrible clanging noises that threaten to break the enamel. The chuckling drones on, throaty and hoarse like a bullfrog.

His fingers slide through the gaps. Long, jagged and broken nails fumble for the lock in a manic attempt at opening the door. He keeps laughing. It's dark, wicked. He knows he's won.

A half-snapped fingernail hits the lock. It spins a bit; the little metal rod moves. A centimeter? Two? It's too many regardless. Frantically, he continues to jab at the lock. His wild, sadistic eyes are locked onto your body as he rams his own into the door. The metal creaks angrily as the heft of his body hits it.

Suddenly, the sound of car tires rolling over branches and gravel outside causes him to stiffen. His hand slinks away, his head tilts back up, vanishing behind the beige metal door. For a moment, all is quiet.

Something blocks out the light above you. Trembling, you lift your eyes and slink down against the porcelain. Towering, his frame peers over the top of the stall. Those wickedly gleeful eyes became soulless, hollow. Angry. He locks gazes with you then backs away. With heavy footfalls, he stomps out of the bathroom until his motions are drowned out by the chatter of other humans. Of conversations and life.

You slowly set your foot down onto solid ground and open the stall door. Your phone falls from your lap, hits the tile and cracks along the side of the screen. The two newcomers look at you with confusion.

"You okay?"

You look around with confusion. "You didn't see him?"

"See... who?"

"The tall guy? With the creepy smile? He was... just here. You *had* to walk by him... to... are you sure?"

They share concerned glances. One shakes their head.

"Nobody's here but us."

You breathe out a quick sigh of relief and hastily move to the sink to slake your dehydration. The newcomers watch you with worry as you wipe the liquid from your chin. You feel hoarse and probably look absolutely deranged. Your hands are shaking, unsteady and weak. In the midst of the panic, you forgot the reason you stopped here in the first place. As you calm down you realize you've wet yourself and feel your cheeks flush with red-hot embarrassment.

This night couldn't get any worse.

As you turn to address them, apologize for the frightened reaction, you stiffen.

You see the yellow eyes in the shadows.

"You-"

Their head falls to the ground with a squelch, mouth agape mid-sentence and eyes wide with lifeless fear. Your face is hit with a spray of warm, fresh blood that drips down onto your t-shirt. The sound of a horrible, bloodcurdling scream echoes out into the night before the still-living stranger is ripped out of the doorway into the night.

Curling, those long, jagged hands wrap around the bathroom entrance. The piercing eyes peer at you through the darkness. Your phone begins to trill frantically as the barrage of messages you sent out into the universe finally reach their destinations. All you can do is swallow hard and watch as his frame eclipses the tall street light before the dingy, once-white walls of the rest stop become painted red with gore and death.

Yes, you should have kept going.

The Fledgling

Dan B. Fierce

This evil clown outfit was the best investment I've ever made.

Preening in the marked-up mirror of the men's room, I adjusted my disguise, making sure I could see through the eyeholes of the latex mask. It made me sweat, having to wear it in the dead of summer, but it would be easy to ditch it if I needed to. At least seventeen other people were wearing similar costumes. Magnificent cover. It was perfect. What better way to blend into this crowd?

The last convention I hit was a huge success. I managed to get a couple of grand in cash as well as several credit cards. Purses were trickier, the contents more unpredictable. But I do love a challenge. Any place I can cover up my looks and stalk around unnoticed, it's a few hours of easy change. I was taught not to stay in one place too long. That increases the chance of getting pinched. A few hours in and I'm a ghost.

Oh sure, I could make an honest living doing sleight-of-hand tricks entertaining the kiddos, but pickpocketing takes more skill. Besides, who wants to be surrounded by a bunch of snot-nosed curtain climbers?

The endorphins were already kicking in. Anticipation danced on my spine. The very air was electric. I couldn't help but smile at my reflection, even if it was covered by painted rubber.

I am a goddamn genius.

I tested the holes where my shorts pockets were underneath the outfit. I could reach them easily enough to stash my loot. The rest of my clothes under the costume were innocuous enough, should I also need to shed the disguise. I had scouted entrances and exits. I knew where the security cameras were and their blind spots. Everything checked out. I was ready.

People feel safe here; they let down their guard easily. Purses and pockets alike, all open for business: my business. It's showtime.

Stepping onto the horror convention floor, I looked for potential victims. A weeping mother was surrounded by officers attempting to comfort her. Something about her baby going missing.

Not my problem. Keeps security busy, though.

A small boy bumped into me. Cute kid, once you got past the sharp, beak-like nose. His blue, smiling eyes traveled up until our gazes met. Then they withered to terror in an instant, his happy face now trembling. I wiggled my fingers. His bottom lip quivered, and the waterworks started.

Oh, great. Here we go.

Panicking, I tried to convince the little imp I was a good guy. Didn't want any undue attention from the cops.

I suppose his mother didn't, either, under the circumstances. One second, the boy was alone, and the next, she was there, shooting me an apologetic look which caught me off-guard. I blinked, dumbstruck.

Where had she come from?

"He's hungry. I haven't fed him in a while." Her fine blonde hair matched her boy's, as did her prominent nose. I watched as she pulled him in for a hug and rocked him, shushing his whimpers until they subsided. "Come on. Let's go get you someone to eat."

"I have to go potty," he chirped.

I watched as she led him down the hall. Then I noticed her designer bag and smiled.

Bingo. She'll be busy. Easy pickings.

Under the seizure-inducing strobe of the fluorescents, I could see the door to the bathroom slowly whisper shut. I checked both ways before entering. Cracking the door, I could hear them talking in the handicapped-accessible stall. I quietly snuck inside. The points of the child's little shoes faced hers. The cubicle door had been closed but not latched. Her bag hung over the entry, begging me to come closer.

A gurgling sound built within the stall. The mother's feet spasmed. I heard the burbling again, making me swallow back my rising gorge. The noise almost made me feel guilty about choosing them. Almost.

Is she sick?

Catching myself beginning to speak, I thought better of it and bent down, leering under the wall. I couldn't register what I saw. My mind had to be playing tricks. Surely it was the angle I was looking from.

Why do her ankles look like they're pointed in an odd direction?

I approached, now more curious than intent on thievery. The retching came to a full crescendo behind the barricade. A rich, sulphuric odor wafted out, filling the room, accompanied by chugging and gulping. My hand covered my nose to keep out the putrid stench.

"There you go." The woman's voice was throaty now, as if her neck were clogged. It reverberated in my skull. "Eat up."

I could see the boy tamp his feet in excitement and heard him swallow deeply.

What the hell are they doing? What is she feeding him?

I paused, bringing myself back into focus on the task at hand. They were distracted. I could do this and then disappear.

Now or never.

Cautiously, I reached toward her purse strap, ready to run off with the prize. As I did, the stall door creaked open. Unable to stop myself from looking, my mind reeled at what I saw.

In front of me was a tall, hunched creature, spindly legs bent backward with the knees pointing to the ceiling. The mother thing's stick-like arms were twice the length of her contorted body. A balloon-shaped head ended in a maw yawning impossibly wide, stuck over the boy's noggin as if testing to see if he'd fit. All action halted. I began to tremble. Her head folded backward to look at me. She stood upright, drool flying and head nearly bumping the water-stained ceiling tiles. A shrill, unearthly screech met my intrusion.

I had been caught before, but this?

The boy, his mouth still stretched wide, peeked past his parent to see what was going on. A pair of slimy, mucus-coated infant's legs hung lifelessly from his mouth. Pieces of flesh and material melted to the floor with a splatter. With an upwards toss of his head, he slurped the limbs down like noodles, neck lumping as the meal moved into his gullet.

My brain vibrated. I felt my bladder loosen. I screamed.

What are they?

"You're interrupting my snack!" His voice was far more menacing than a six-year-old's should have been, invading my head. His stomach distended outward, the contents being quickly digested as they sloshed about inside.

Eyes wide, my pupils dilated in horror. My heart hammered in my ribcage; my mind was unable to wrap itself around this sight, this unholy family before me. Knees threatening to buckle, I slowly backed away.

I tried to play off my presence as an accident, apologizing for the invasion. My voice cracked through a dry throat. Sweat beaded my forehead. I assured them I saw nothing, but I don't know whether I was trying to convince the two of them or myself.

Go. I have to go. I have to get out of here. I have to-

"I'm still hungry," the boy-thing grumbled, loud enough to shake the mirrors above the sinks. His once baby blue eyes were the soulless coal black of a frenzied shark's. He followed me with famished eyes, his pointed tongue tracing his contorted lips. I could see the muscles in his tiny legs clinch, an apex predator readying for the pounce.

I spun to escape, slipping on the urine-slicked flooring. Charging me with his frog-like mouth wide open and eager, he clamped down on my leg. I yowled in pain and surprise. He worried his head back and forth like a dog with a squeaky toy. The fabric of my outfit shredded, and small needles scraped my leg enough to dig in and draw blood. Fireworks burst behind my eyelids. Every one of my nerves caught fire, starting at his bite. I batted at the hellspawn, trying to pry him loose.

Get off of me, you parasite!

The mother screeched at my assault, clambering over the stall divider like an insect, eyes trained on me. My arm froze in terror mid-strike.

"Don't touch my child!" she bellowed, the impact of her demand hitting me like a gust from rancid roadkill. She plopped to the ground, her pinprick legs clacking on the tile. She roared inches away from my face, withering away any courage I may have had left. My entire body quaked, eyes squinted shut as tight as I could get them.

Please don't hurt me. Please don't hurt me.

Sensing my resistance was gone, her unearthly face softened, glancing at her offspring. "No, sweetie," instructed the mother-thing patiently, causing the boy to let go. "You don't have your big boy teeth yet." She patted his head as he looked up at her, intent on learning. "You'll have to take smaller bites of someone this big. Savor your kill. Enjoy it."

Every muscle in my body suddenly locked up.

Why can't I move? Help!

The mom-thing looked at me with her hideous face. Sunken eyes bore into my soul. She may have even been smiling as she spoke to me, her mouth unmoving.

"He may not have much of a bite, but his venom will keep you alive while he feeds." Her feet ticked on the tile around me as she paced, looking me over hungrily like a suckling pig. "The good news is; you won't feel it as I tear your flesh off." Her elongated, bony hands grabbed one of mine, the offending one that had punched at her progeny.

"I think it's only fitting we start here," the abomination cooed. "Don't you?"

Her claims that I'd be numb were a lie. I felt every bit of pain as that thing bent my forearm, snapping it like kindling, splintered bone jutting through my skin. The agony was so intense, it caused the air to leave my lungs. Blood spurted from my wound. Sinew snapped, and flesh tore until my limb was no longer mine. Her tongue flicked out, covering my gushing injury with a thick, acrid saliva which burned and halted the bleeding.

"Can't have you dying yet," she mocked. "Where's the fun in that?"

Her immense maw opened again as her tongue teased and vined around my severed hand before she tilted her head back and dropped it down her throat. The boy peeped like a hatchling in its nest, his arms flapping with starved excitement.

I could hear her stomach roiling again, her child licking his chops impatiently. I think she maneuvered in front of me deliberately so I could watch a piece of my body, slicked from bile, slid from her mouth into the kid's.

"More!" The little bastard chewed ever so slightly before swallowing. "He tastes funny." One final gulp, and it was over. "But I like it."

"You have to finish your plate."

No. He really doesn't.

Tears began to trickle down my cheeks. A whimper escaped my mouth. Mother approached once more, her ungodly face gawking, deciding which part to take next. With a hellish roar, she swiped at me, her claws paring my clothes from me like a banana peel. Rivulets opened up on my chest where her infernal touch had sliced me open.

"Here, baby," she soothed at her son, "Let me help."

Sticking one of her harpy-like talons inside me, she hooked a strip of skin and muscle loose on my torso. It hung like a flag, flapping in the stale breeze from the air conditioner. Her offspring snapped onto it, pulling like a terrier on a rope. White hot agony filled every inch of me while he unraveled me. He yanked free the strip of flesh, gulping it down.

Stop! Please stop.

My pleas echoed in the small space. No one came to help. I didn't exist outside of the door. The contraction of my diaphragm made my insides shift. A grayish bloody tube emerged from within me I fought my frozen neck to tilt my head down. It was my intestines.

The boy dove at me when my insides relocated. He pecked and tore and swallowed. He fattened. I lost substance. His head drilled deeper within me until all I could see was his lower half kicking for further purchase. My body shook and rocked while he ate. The ravenous smacking of lips accompanied a sloppy, wet sound while my inner cavity was ravaged. Gravity embraced me, my body plopping to the floor, rattling my skeleton.

"Don't eat so fast," the demonic matriarch instructed. "You'll get a tummy ache." I felt one.

Sinking Sally

Ashley Watson

"You're such a wimp, Jaden."

I rolled my eyes at Margie's snarkiness. We had been best friends for years, but sometimes I just wanted to punch her in the face. "Then why don't you go do it if you're so brave

She rolled her eyes back. "I told you I already did it last week at my grandma's house, and she didn't show up."

"Then why do you want me to do it so bad?"

"Because she might show up for you."

"She" being Sinking Sally. The legend of Sally is that she was a victim of sexual assault. After the attack happened, she tried to get help from anyone she could: family, friends, the police, and literally anyone she thought would listen. No one believed her because the man who supposedly hurt her was an upstanding community member, but it's never been confirmed who the man was. Everyone turned against her for the scandalous lie they thought she had conjured up for attention, even her family. And so, she killed herself. She drowned herself in a bathtub, and the legend of Sinking Sally was born.

I sighed dramatically and rolled my eyes once more as I stood up from the couch. Fear was coursing through every vein in my body, but I wasn't going to let her know that. And really, if nothing happened to her, then why would it to me? Clearly, it wasn't real, but I couldn't shake the fear away.

After I went in there, I shut the door behind me. I pulled the crumpled sheet of notebook paper Margie had given me out of my pocket. It was the list of rules for the summoning ritual handwritten by one of her other friends. Just as the paper stated, I filled the bathtub halfway full and lit all 6 of the candles Margie had given me before placing them around the tub. Their flowery smells mingled in the small bathroom, and I took a deep breath of them to calm my nerves. The only sound was the faucet's methodical dripping.

"I don't hear anything happening!" yelled Margie. "Did she get you already?"

She flew into a fit of giggles as if me dying was the most hilarious joke in the world to her. I rolled my eyes and ignored her. Friendships with Margie involved a lot of eye rolls. I reread the chant on the paper. It had to be sung, and I'm embarrassed to say that a part of me was also anxious because I knew Margie would be making fun of my singing in the future, even if it seemed rather trivial at the moment. I couldn't help but notice the shakiness of the words, as if whoever wrote it was scared Sally would be summoned then and there. I felt even shakier than the words were, but I ignored that as well, and took another deep breath. I did a double-check to make sure I had everything correct.

"Oh!" I called out as I realized the mirror wasn't covered. I sprang to my feet, grabbed a towel from the cabinet, and threw it over the mirror's ornate frame. I tried not to think about the terrified expression present on my face or the fact that it might possibly be replaced by something sinister in a few moments.

It's not real, I thought. *Don't be scared.*

I turned out the lights, kneeled before the bathtub, took another deep breath for good measure, and began to sing:

Sinking Sally, serenade
Through the water, retrograde

Use my energy, ebb and flow
So that you will surely show

After I finished, the room was silent once more. I sat there for a minute in the darkness, almost hoping something would occur. I felt stupid after a few moments, though, so I stood up from my perch on the floor. The candles flickering in the darkness cast shadows on the wall that were beginning to make me uncomfortable, so I went ahead and turned on the light. I tried to open the door, but it wouldn't budge.

I jiggled it, wondering how it could be locked when the lock was on the inside. The doorknob itself was also moving and clearly not broken. I pushed against the door with all of my body weight, knowing full well that if Margie was holding it closed, I was stronger than her and could push her off. But none of these possibilities seemed to be happening: the door just wouldn't open.

I began to jiggle it more forcefully, hoping and praying that it would magically open. It still refused, however, and I felt bile slowly rising up my throat. I swallowed it as I heard the water begin to lap against the tub. I banged on the door, calling for Margie to come help even though I knew logically that she couldn't be the cause of this. My pleading went ignored by Margie, but it was noticed by whatever was splashing around in the tub behind me. It scraped against the tub's sides as it released a throaty chuckle.

"Margie, please!" it mimicked, sounding eerily identical to me. "Please let me out!" It chuckled once more before giving me an order. "Turn around."

My trembling body refused to move, frozen in fear. I was scared I would throw up again and be unable to prevent myself from choking.

"I said..." it began, "TURN AROUND!"

At once, my body moved of its own volition, snapping around and marching towards the tub like a toy soldier.

It laughed again, giving me a sinister grin. "Now, that's better."

Tears began to stream down my face at the sight before me.

"Take it from me: you should really pick better friends, girly," she said as she flicked a strand of hair out of my face with a swollen and decaying finger. My inability to move was the only thing keeping me from gagging from her smell. However, it did not stop my body from its involuntary quaking. I understood exactly why my body was afraid; Sally was a hulking mass of waterlogged rotten flesh. Her whole body looked puffy and gray, and the few strands of hair she had left on her hair were bleached as if she had been in the sun for ages. She gave me a smile full of blackened teeth.

In a motion so quick my eyes couldn't even register it properly, her face was suddenly inches from mine. How her body looked so fragile, yet could pull off feats of this nature was otherworldly. But, of course, it was. I had been told everything I needed to know about Sally, yet I had been too stupid to believe it. The being standing before me was not a silly urban legend. She was horrifyingly real.

She wrapped her hands around my face, shoving my cheeks in towards my mouth. Her claw-like fingers dug into my skin and made me wince. She tilted my head this way and that, eyeing me like an interesting specimen before shrugging.

"This one will do, I guess," she said before her eyes widened.

They became milky white as her fingers forcefully tore open my mouth, spreading it open as far as it could go. Her mouth mirrored mine as a deep croak tore from her throat. It sounded painful, but her face remained blank. A wispy smoke filtered from her mouth and crawled into mine. Then, although her disgusting hands remained wrapped around my lips, I felt something begin to suffocate me.

It wasn't until I felt a bone-chilling cold overwhelm my body, inside and out, that I realized it wasn't suffocating me; it was taking over me. As the wisp traveled throughout my body, I quaked from the freezing cold. The pain began in patches across my body before spanning out, engulfing me in searing pain as the smoke spread out completely. It was difficult to explain how, but all of these sensations were combined into one big mind-shattering experience. I wasn't even sure I still had the brain activity necessary to comprehend my state or the words to describe it. As my vision began to dim and blur around the edges, I tried to cry out, but the force of the smoke entering me was too powerful. The rest of my vision faded completely until all I saw was black, and I felt like I had shriveled up into nothingness. And then, there was complete and total nothingness as I felt myself lose touch with reality and fizzle out of existence.

**

I released a shuddering gasp before I stood up from the floor, my head pounding from the collision it made with the tiles. My eyes squinted due to the bright lights hurting them. I hadn't been in an actual body in what felt like ages. Earthly bodies had more strict limitations than spirit ones, and the difference was hitting me heavily. The pressure of gravity felt suffocating at first, but was now subsiding. Even the ginormous amount of memories she had stored in her head was hard to process, and I'm not even quite sure how I had been the one to keep them.

After a few minutes, I could open my watery eyes to look at myself in the mirror. I wiped away the tears from my now youthful cheeks, admiring the golden hues in my hair and eyes. Sound had not yet come back to me, at least not fully. Its effects gradually increased while I got used to the world again. However, as I turned on the sink and let the water trickle onto my fingers, sound came back in full force.

A loud bashing on the door made me fling my body to the left. I let out a gasp, and my hand gripped my chest. I felt my rapidly beating heart under my palm. Margie's screams finally entered my ears. "Jaden, are you okay? Please answer me!" Her voice sounded hoarse as if she had been screaming for a while.

I quickly opened the door to shut her up and gave her my biggest grin. "Hi. I'm fine."

Her look of shock softened a bit but remained. Her hand stayed frozen mid-door-pound as well. "Why didn't you answer for so long?"

"I was still scared." Flashes of the fear Jaden felt because of me hit me, making my heartbeat increase. I hid my discomfort from Margie, though.

As she dropped her hand, a tinge of confusion glimmered in her doe-like eyes. "D-did you fall? I heard a crash."

I waved a hand dismissively. "Oh, yeah. I've been a bit clumsy lately."

Margie's shoulders slumped. I could tell my nonchalant attitude made her feel embarrassed and as if she had overreacted. Her gullible innocence reminded me of myself before I was defiled. I couldn't wait to have revenge, but for now, I had to play the part of Jaden.

I took a step towards her as a way to say I wanted to get out of the bathroom. She staggered backward and almost fell, and that's when I noticed the reason she was now avoiding my eyes wasn't from embarrassment. I'm not sure how, but she could tell something was different. She wasn't as oblivious as I thought.

"I told you it was just a silly superstition. You don't have anything to worry about," I lied with a devilish grin.

"But I'll have to do something about you," I thought.

Musca Domestica

Julia C. Lewis

The hot stream of water from the shower feels glorious on my aching bones. For days now, I've been battling symptoms of a bad cold and with it, the accompanying body aches. As the room fills up with steam and the smell of eucalyptus aromatherapy tablet, I let myself relax with my eyes closed. I try not to think of all the work that's been piling up in my email inbox. When I snuck a quick glance at it this morning, I saw several emails marked *urgent. This sinus headache is way more urgent than your request, Susan,* I thought as I slammed the laptop shut. I hadn't called in sick for nothing. Begrudgingly, I had dragged myself out of bed and into the shower. A decision I am now grateful for as the hot water helps me feel better than I have in days. I take a deep breath and inhale the steam.

Thump.

I open my eyes as a curious thumping sound followed by a splash cuts through the silence in the bathroom. The room is tiny, with barely enough room for the shower, toilet and sink, which makes any noise sound way louder than it should. The room's lack of a window was the first negative thing I noticed when I moved in. Goosebumps pimple my arms as I peek my head out of the teal shower curtain and check the room.

Nothing.

I close the curtain and let myself relax again, this time trying to think about my upcoming vacation with my mom. Both of us have been excited for our mother-daughter cruise for over a year now. I smile at the thought of us drinking cocktails in the sun.

Thump!

The sound comes again, only this time more violent and urgent. I pop my head out of the curtain and stare at the closed toilet lid. It's rattling, almost as if someone is pushing up against it from within the toilet bowl. *I'm hallucinating. No way is there something strong enough* in *my toilet to make this kind of impact.* I flinch and almost slip in the shower as the lid rises an inch. Without thinking about it, I jump out of the shower and plant my naked, wet body on top of the toilet lid, sliding uncomfortably on the cold plastic. *What the hell?*

Beneath my body, the thing in the toilet bowl becomes agitated and starts violently smacking against the lid. With each slam I flinch, unable to comprehend the insane situation I find myself in. Sure, I've seen people have all sorts of critters in their toilets, but that's on the internet. It's too cold for snakes where I live and you don't get frogs in your pipes in the middle of a big city. No, whatever this is, isn't a lost animal, this is something malicious.

***

I've been sitting on the toilet for what seems like hours. The water is steadily running in the shower, but it's no longer steamy in the room. I'm guessing the water ran cold at least an hour ago, so all I'm doing is wasting precious resources. I don't even want to think of my next water bill. After frantically rioting a few more times, the mysterious thing in my toilet has stopped. For now. Yet, I'm terrified to get up. I'm too scared of it simply lying in wait and popping out as soon as I relent. I push my frizzy, dry hair out of my eyes and bury my face into my hands. I'm exhausted.

"Wha-," I start drowsily, just before I'm thrown to the side and hit my head painfully on the shower wall. "Fuck!"

Next to me the toilet lid opens with a jerk and something small flies out of it and zips through the room. It looks like a normal fly, the one that flies drowsily through your house on a summer's day, occasionally bumping into windows with an aggravated *buzz*. The only difference is this one is neon yellow in color. It looks toxic. Nevertheless, I laugh uncomfortably at the thought that I'd been afraid of this tiny fly for hours and held myself captive in my own bathroom because of it.

My legs shake from prolonged sitting as I get up, my head pounding where I hit it. I turn off the water in the shower and reach for the doorknob. That's when two things happen simultaneously: First, I realize the door is stuck shut and second, the fly smacks me in the back of the head with an audible *slap*, causing me to hit my forehead on the wood. I try the door again but realize that it won't open no matter how hard I pull; the humidity from the shower must have made the ancient wood swell up. I'm trapped.

The fly comes in for a second attack and I clumsily try to avoid it, ducking down and in the process slipping on a puddle. *I hate this tiny bathroom!* As I fall to the ground, I open my mouth to scream and in one calculated swoop, the fly flies into my mouth and down my throat.

***

I used to think that there was nothing worse than next-day hangover puking, but now I know better. Nothing will ever be as gross as my attempt to purge this neon fly from my body. My whole body is shaking and I'm a crumpled mess beside the toilet. I keep praying, hoping, wishing that someone will drop by my apartment uninvited, which is something I would usually hate, but would welcome with open arms today. Just someone knocking on my door, seeing if I am ok. Maybe they could hear my cries and screams outside in the hallway. I don't care if it's my mom trying to guilt-trip me in not visiting enough or even my landlord asking for more rent. I simply *need* someone to rescue me from this bizzaro nightmare.

At this point, I have no idea how long I've been stuck in my bathroom. I have tried the door a few more times, but it's as if someone has superglued it shut- it won't budge at all. My phone has been ringing faintly from my bedroom a few times, but no one seems worried enough to show up in person or send the police. I realize it's just me in here, and well, the fly inside my body.

One good thing about being locked inside your bathroom, and not, let's say your bedroom, is that you have unlimited water. I'm glad I don't have to worry about dehydration at this point, even though the fly is making it hard to keep water down. And even though I've wrapped myself in a bath towel for a makeshift dress, I've been mentally kicking myself for not keeping a laundry hamper in here. Oh, how I would love some comfy, if dirty, sweatpants right now. Anything would do.

I can feel the fly inside my body. It's moving around, first in my stomach, then my throat and finally somehow behind my eyes. I wasn't the best in biology, but even I know that it shouldn't be able to move around like that, let alone still be alive. I scratch my skin as I feel it landing and crawling on my various organs, tickling the nerves behind my eyeballs. At first, I tried to ignore the sensation, telling myself it was all in my head. But in reality, it's the fly inside my head, which is causing me to majorly panic. I throw myself against the bathroom door again and again, hoarsely screaming for help...

It doesn't help.

***

It's whispering to me now. Telling me to let it out, that I should help it escape my body. I feel its tiny wings fluttering against my brain, tickling me. It's a godawful sensation and I shake my head wildly in an attempt to make it move. *Buzz, buzz, buzz* it goes. Around and around my head.

I clench my hair in my fists and scream in frustration. "GET OUT!"

The fly keeps buzzing and laughs at me from deep within my left ear canal. It beats its wings against my eardrum, giving me terrible vertigo. With my eyes closed, I stagger to the sink, gripping it hard until my fingers ache. "Leave me alone!" I shake my head wildly, like a rabid dog. Spittle flies from my lips and mixes with the tears streaming out of my eyes.

I jerk my head up, as I feel something brushing against my eyelashes. There, in the mirror I can see the fly peeking from behind my eye lid. It's waving its tiny feet at me, playing a sick game of peek-a-boo. Quickly, I slap my eye with my hand, causing nothing but a stinging sensation; the fly is nowhere in sight.

Out of nowhere, I think back to a documentary I've watched before. The fact that flies are capable of laying up to a hundred and fifty eggs a day fills my thoughts. The world around me goes dark as I think about the fly sprinkling the inside of my body with its eggs, making me a human incubator for its vile, neon offspring.

"Noooooo!" I shout in despair and face the bathroom door, shaking it, pounding on it, screaming from the depths of my strained lungs. "LET ME OUT!"

We'll make a lovely family, I imagine the fly whispering with a big grin on its face.

Defeated, I slide to the floor, my back against the door. *It's useless, unless...*

I glance at the open shelf under my sink, a pair of nail scissors gleaming in the artificial light of my bathroom. *Yes,* I think, *this will work fine.*

The tile feels cool as I crawl towards the scissors and pick them up. I pull myself up with the help of the sink and grip them tightly. Facing the mirror, I raise the scissors to my eye and take a deep breath.

"This might hurt both of us, fly."

A Barrel of Teeth and a Barrel of Laughs

Wesley Winters

Another eighty minutes gone, another pee break to interrupt my dreaming. I'm sick of not sleeping through the night. Sometimes, I can't be sure what is real. Lately, I dream of my teeth falling out and filling my mouth with marbles that click and clack over one another as I try breathing through their masses.

Rarely does my partner stir. She must be used to my bathroom breaks. That or she's a heavy sleeper. We haven't been together very long for me to be sure. She woke a few times the first week she stayed over but not again since. What I do know is she makes it through the night without interruption, unlike myself. I'm so tired all the time now.

This has been going on for several months, ever since my employer started downsizing. A lot of my friends have been fired recently. I worry about being next and losing my house. I've read that dreams of losing your teeth mean you fear a loss of control. I have no doubt why I'm having these dreams, all things considered. My quality of life hangs in the balance! And coupled with this frequent urination, I'm becoming a bit more concerned. I don't think I've ever heard of bladder problems tied to anxiety, but it sounds plausible. I know my intestines knot whenever I'm stressed.

I've stopped drinking after six in the evening in hopes that it will stop my overnight trips to bathroom, but it hasn't seemed to make a difference. And I'm always thirsty before bed, which makes this all the harder. Last week, I had a UTI that took days to recover from, and that was with antibiotics from the doctor. It's not even my first this year. Or second or third. The doctor said it's strange for me to be getting them at all because males don't often suffer from such infections. I pee after sex and drink lots of water but still I suffer from these fucking things every few weeks or so.

At 5:03, my bladder wakes me for the third time since going to bed at 11. It's my day off, so I should be able to stay in bed later than normal. But every time I have to use the bathroom, I have to go through the process of falling asleep all over again. That doesn't come easily for me. I usually end up lying awake until the next time my bladder begins to ache, right as I'm drifting back to sleep.

When I go to wash my hands, I inspect my teeth in the mirror. That has become a new habit thanks to the dreams. I'm trying to decide if I've really used the bathroom or just dreamt it. That's been happening a lot, too. It's like when you do something repetitive at work so often that you dream of doing your job at night. It's insufferable, like you just can't escape something.

My teeth appear fine for the moment, as do my gums. I go ahead and brush them as part of my morning routine; it's probably too late to bother returning to bed at this point. Amy will be up within the hour, so why force my brain into another sleep cycle I won't be able to finish? Then I'd have to drag my ass through four hours of exhaustion as I wait for my brain to reset.

Though I won't be working today, Amy will be giving horse riding lessons until midafternoon. That's her side hustle. From Monday to Friday, she manages the office of a home inspection company. She's usually up with an alarm around

6am during the weekend. With the time I have until then, I decide to make us breakfast. That seems like a nice surprise for her.

I've only been in the kitchen twenty minutes when I feel my bladder ache once more. When I return to the bathroom, I am immediately frightened to see how dark the bags are under my eyes. I swear they weren't like that before. But now they droop dramatically in such a way that they look as fake as a bad movie prop. When I pinch them between my fingers, I am able to hold them by an inch. That can't be right. And my eyes are possibly worse—instead of milky white, they are gray and scratched with red streaks. I turn on the faucet and splash my face several times with water to see if it does any good but my entire face appears to be slouching now, as if I'm wearing an old man mask.

"What the actual fuck?"

I must be dreaming, after all. Just because my teeth aren't falling out yet doesn't mean this isn't just another nightmare. So, I punch the mirror as hard as I can and break the glass. Shards tumble into the sink loudly as I wait to feel the residual pain in my knuckles. There isn't any to be had, which further confirms my sleeping state, as far as I'm concerned. Unsure if I should wake myself or just go about my morning with my face losing miserably to gravity—I need the sleep, after all—I return to the bedroom to check on Amy. Her back is turned to me, her bare shoulder above the covers begging to be touched. When I lay a hand on her, she moans in her sleep.

"Amy, baby?"

I squeeze her shoulder gently and plant a kiss on her temple. Amy rolls over to face me and smiles. When she does, I see her own teeth are jumbled and falling out of her mouth. I curse and recoil several feet without thinking. Then I remind myself this is a dream and that I should relax. But I can't help but wonder what it means when you dream of someone *else's* teeth falling out. I swallow back my surprise and ask Amy if she wants me to bring her breakfast in bed.

"If only you were sleeping better," she says in a mocking tone, sitting up in bed and stretching. "Then maybe you'd realize what's been in front of you all this time."

I can't help but raise one of my bushy eyebrows that has grown into a caterpillar across my decaying face. "What?"

Amy throws her legs over the bedside and stands. She is naked and vibrant, with the exception of her bloodied mouth. Teeth continue to fall from her lips, far more than she should have. When she holds open her arms to embrace me, I ask her, "What's wrong with you?"

She drops her arms and narrows her eyes at me. "That is the question, isn't it?"

My bladder seems to burst and I squeeze my eyes shut in discomfort. When I open them, I find myself in bed with the room dark. I find my phone and check the time. It's 3:32 in the middle of the night. I feel like I'm going to piss my pants if I don't get to the bathroom quickly. I throw back the covers without regard to Amy's sleeping form beside me, and hurry to the toilet. As I release a stream that is oddly powerful for someone that hasn't had a drink in over eight hours, I hear Amy roll over in bed. She mumbles something in her sleep, then returns to silence. Once I've finished with the toilet, I skip its flushing to keep from waking her. When I turn to the mirror above the sink, I reflectively shut my eyes in fear of what I may see. But when I open them, I look completely normal. Maybe even handsome, despite my bedhead.

"Jesus," I groan as I wash my hands. I tell myself I need help, that the dreams are becoming too hard to distinguish from reality now. I'm having trouble keeping track of when I've actually gotten up for the bathroom and when I've only imagined it. Maybe I should keep a journal to record my nightly visits. During the day, I can check to see what has actually been written versus what I *think* I remember.

As far as I can tell, I manage to return to sleep until Amy's 6 am alarm. When she gets up, so do I. Together, we have breakfast and watch the news. We say very little, but that's normal. By 7, she's eaten, washed, and dressed for work. When she leaves, I collapse onto the couch and consider my options. It is then I remember Amy's own decaying state in my dream, and decide to Google its meaning. One of the top results says that dreams of other people's teeth falling out may represent a fear of that person in your waking life. I laugh aloud and shake my head. I'm not scared of Amy. Why would I be? She's harmless.

I toss my phone aside and turn on HBO. Recently, I've begun rewatching *True Detective*. The first season is brilliant.

When there's a crash outside, I jolt forward and fall from the couch. Had I fallen asleep? Groggily, I stand and go to the window overlooking the street. Outside, a large van has collided into the oak tree out front of the Malinski's house. My emergency response kicks in and I quickly find my shoes to run outside. I'm nearly to the van when I realize I'm only wearing a wifebeater and boxers, but it's too late to worry about it. I reach the driver's side door and go to yank it open when I realize no one is inside the vehicle. I look across the console at the passenger side, then check the backseat. The van is completely empty.

"What did you do?" Pamela screeches from the front door of her house.

I step back from the van and throw my hands out by my sides. "I didn't do shit, Mrs. Malinski. I heard a crash and came to help."

"Get out of my fucking garden, you idiot!" she screams, jabbing her finger my direction and stomping across the lawn.

I look down at my feet and see that I'm standing in the flowers that border her oak tree. Probably worse is the fact that there's no longer a crashed van there. I jump back from the garden and curse under my breath, sure that I must be dreaming again. Pamela reaches me a second later and smashes her finger against my chest with enough force to push me back a step.

"You're a bum, Charles. Drunk again, I assume?"

A *bum*? Yeah, I must be dreaming again.

"I don't drink, Mrs. Malinski," I say, moving backwards toward the road. Even if this isn't reality, I don't want to be around her any longer than I have to be.

"And that slutty girlfriend of yours is just as bad," Pamela continues, her finger forever sticking into my chest. "I've seen her up and about all hours of the fuckin' night!"

I pause, confused. "Doing what?" I ask, mere inches from the sidewalk.

"Coming and going, coming and going!"

I sigh and turn away from my neighbor to cross the street. "I'll be heading home now," I say without looking back. A moment later, I hear Pamela by her flowerbed cursing up a storm under her breath.

Back inside, I consider going to the bathroom—a new habit of mine, you see—but realize I don't need to go. Happy with this discovery, I return to the couch and look for a movie to watch. Hours pass by, some of which must have been dreamt, I'm sure, not that I can tell any difference. A good chunk of the day is lost in the void, though, that much I know, because suddenly Amy is coming through the front door. I check the time and see it is 3:32 in the afternoon. Something about that strikes me as odd but I don't know why.

"Have you just been lying there all day?" she asks upon seeing me on the couch in my robe.

"I suppose this one got away from me," I begin to explain, feeling defensive. "I've been off and on sleeping. You know that's something I'm having trouble with."

"So, you say." She drops off her things and heads into the kitchen for a drink. I stand and follow her to the fridge.

"You know what Mrs. Malinski said to me today?" I ask her.

She shrugs and opens a beer. "What?"

"She said she sees you all night, inside and outside the house."

Amy smiles and says, "And?"

I'm surprised and I'm sure it shows. "Wait. Really?"

"Really *what*?"

"You're up all night?"

"Sometimes. Haven't you noticed?"

"You'd think, what with my endless bathroom breaks."

"Your what?"

I study her for a moment, my teeth set tightly in my jaw. She appears to be serious. She has no idea what I'm talking about. "Forget it," I say. "I must be dreaming again, is all."

"What the hell are you talking about?"

I turn away from her and stop beside the couch. I look down at the cushions where there waits a rumpled blanket and the remote. Did I really spend all day in front of the TV? How much of that time was I awake? Am I awake right now?

"Babe, you're acting funny," Amy says, coming up from behind me. "Maybe I can set your mind at ease. Hell, maybe you'll even get some sleep after." She slides a hand around my side and down over my crotch as she drinks her beer over my opposite shoulder. "You game?"

I turn to her and decide a wet dream is better than a dry dream. "Let's go."

In bed, I somehow manage to drift in and out of consciousness as her head bobs between my legs. When I've finished, I only know I have because she sits up and wipes a tissue over her lips. Then she looks at me and smiles. "Did you like that, baby?"

I must have, seeing as I finished, but I don't remember much of it. I put on my best, stupidest grin and tell her she's knocked me out for the count. "Good," she says, getting off the bed. "Try sleeping. See if you can go until morning."

"But it's only four in afternoon," I argue weakly, not really at all interested in staying awake any longer.

"Shhh. Just close your eyes and get some rest. I've got some work to do, anyway."

Before I can ask myself what more she has to do for the day, darkness swallows me whole.

When I wake, the room is dark and the window curtains are pulled. My bladder feels like a stone weighing heavily over my hip. I get out of bed and realize Amy's side is empty. I wonder where she is on my way to the bathroom. Two steps from the bed, I trip and crash against the dresser. I grumble irritably and pick myself back up. After I've peed, I stand in front of the mirror and check the bags under my eyes. They look normal; puffy and shadowed, but normal. I flash myself an actor's smile, but a tooth falls out of my mouth and into the sink. I curse and pick it up for closer examination.

"Shit," I think aloud. I must be dreaming, after all.

Downstairs, I hear the front door open and close. Is that Amy returning or leaving? What time is it?

I look at the tooth again and feel myself waver in place. I don't know if I'm lightheaded or simply that damned tired, but I grip the edges of the sink to steady myself. I blink several times (or maybe a hundred times, I don't know) and realize Amy is suddenly there in the bathroom with me. She's got a busted lip and her hair's a mess.

"What happened to you?" I ask sleepily, trying to turn without falling. Once I've made a full rotation, I rest my backside against the sink with my hands still holding its edges.

Amy looks as if she's been in a fight but she's in good spirits. "The normal," she tells me, reaching over my shoulder for her toothbrush and the toothpaste. "You mind moving aside?"

I inch over to the shower curtain and consider taking a seat on the toilet instead of standing. Before I can make up my mind, Amy says, "You asleep right now?"

I laugh with actual sincerity and tell her, "I have no fucking clue anymore."

"That's good," she says, scrubbing at her teeth with her brush.

"Huh?"

She meets my gaze in the mirror, then spits into the sink. When she raises her head once more, her teeth spill from her lips and into the bowl. When she turns to face me, she's holding her toothbrush around its middle with the bristles tickling the space between her thumb and index finger. Though her teeth are magically back in place, her smile continues to unnerve me.

"What are you doing?" I ask with a hand pressed against the wall behind me. I still feel unsteady on my feet, like every blink is taking me between a dream state and an awakened state.

Amy lifts her toothbrush and plunges its rounded (yet pointy) end into my eye. I swear I see an explosion of stars when it happens. My body goes rigid, as if I've had some sort of stroke or electric shock, and I beg myself to wake. But when I try to blink myself back to reality, I am unable to close my left eye because THERE'S A FUCKING TOOTHBRUSH IN IT.

So, I scream.

Amy yanks her makeshift weapon out of my eye and grabs the side of my head by the hair. Before I can guess what comes next, she swings me into the shower curtain with a strength I did not know she possessed. I pull the curtain down with me into the tub and yelp in surprise. The pain has yet to come, but I hope that's because this is just the wildest dream I've had in recent memory. As I fight with the curtain wrapped around my body, I continue to blink the only eye I have left. One second, Amy is standing over the tub with a busted lip, the next she has her mouth open and her teeth are pouring out like a waterfall onto me.

"What the fuck is going on?" I howl, kicking my feet and trying to stand in the tub.

Instead of the bloody toothbrush, Amy is now holding my shaving razor. She leans over me and swipes the head of the razor over my forehead at an awkward angle, cutting me. I curse from the sting and realize I can actually feel pain again. My eye is throbbing dully, deep inside my skull, and there's blood trickling down my cheek from the gouged socket. I yell for Amy to stop attacking me, but she swipes me again with the razor, this time cutting my cheek and then my nose. She must know this will take forever to do me in but I think she's having fun. I need to make her stop by force.

I roll myself out of the tub and land hard at her feet. Amy laughs and slams the side of her fist into the mirror, shattering it. When I look up at her, teeth fall from the sky and pelt me in the face.

Blink.

Blink.

Blink!

I'm becoming desperate. If even a moment of this is real, something entirely fucked is taking place between me and Amy. I grab her ankle and pull. She falls at an awkward angle against the toilet, but she's already snagged a shard of glass from the sink. She brings it down on my shoulder like a knife, piercing me several inches deep. I scream—yeah, the pain is really there now—and ask her why she's doing this.

"Because, Charles," she says through excited gasps for air, "this is what I do, baby."

She stabs me again and again until I relinquish her ankle and slump backwards against the side of the tub. Then she stands over me and shakes her head. "You've been so sleep-deprived, you haven't seen a thing wrong with me this entire time. I honestly wonder just how much of our relationship was a dream to you. What do you remember of today? Yesterday? Last week? Do you even remember how we met?"

I'm losing consciousness, and this time it's not because I'm tired. I think it's because I'm dying.

"I straight up told you I kill people for fun. On our *first fucking* date. And you practically had me move in later that week." She laughs and inspects the bloody mirror fragment in her hand. "You want to know something else? I've framed you for half a dozen murders in the past month alone. Your boss is about to fire you because you keep missing work, and the house payment is two months overdue. Your neighbors think you're crazy because you blast music off and on throughout the day—you're welcome—and there's lights on all hours of the night. I've stashed drugs in various spots around your house, all of which are easy to find. And there's a document prominently saved on your desktop that journals your bathroom breaks and your waning sanity. No one is even going to question your death! It's going to be ruled as suicide the moment you're tied to those murders and the cops come breaking down the door."

My head dips time and again as she talks. Finally, I manage to lift it defiantly and look her in the eye. "They'll know about you, Amy. People have been seeing you here for weeks."

"Have they, though?" she asks.

I blink but the darkness is overpowering. My vision is primarily exploding starbursts now, but I shake my head repeatedly to get a grip on the bathroom once more. When I do, I find myself alone, bleeding against the side of the tub with mirror shards scattered about my feet. Somewhere in the house, I hear Metallica blaring. And in my hand is a rotted tooth from my mouth.

I can't help but wonder...

Did Amy ever exist?

Life Alert

Kay Hanifen

"Help, I've fallen, and I can't get up!" You used to make fun of those Life Alert commercials with the poor acting and quotable hook. But then you got old. Your footsteps became unsteady and uncertain. Slipping on wet tile in the bathroom wasn't always so dangerous, but when you fell, you heard something crack in your hip. And you live alone. No one heard you scream. Now, you're lying on your side and even *trying* to move the right half of your body sends shockwaves of agony through you. And you're naked as the day you were born, shivering as the cold tiles and water drying from your skin saps the warmth from your body. Should've invested in that damn Life Alert.

Okay, don't panic. What was that quote from the book series your grandson loves? "Fear is the mind killer. Fear is the little death that brings total oblivion." Repeat that mantra in your head like a prayer. You stopped believing in God a long time ago, but a real prayer couldn't hurt. A prayer that someone will notice you're missing before it's too late. A prayer that you won't die naked on the bathroom floor. Of all the ways to go.

It seems like God has a sense of humor, though, because as you're praying, your front door opens, and you hear hushed voices coming from downstairs.

Your daughter lives an hour away and your son across the country. There is no way it can be either of them, especially at this hour. You don't usually shower at midnight, but the local rotary club was hosting a sock hop and auction to raise money to help repair the library after an electrical fire and you were manning the drinks. You didn't even get back until 11:30, and even though the doctor said not to, you had a drink to relax before getting into the shower. Sure, your medication makes alcohol hit you harder, but you should have been sober enough to manage taking a shower and getting ready for bed.

Now, you have a choice. You can gamble with the friendliness of these intruders and call for help or stay silent and pray that they leave without finding you. There is a difference between thieves and killers, and most people who steal will not murder. They can be your one chance at survival.

But the memory of watching that old Kubrick movie, *A Clockwork Orange*, flashes before your mind unbidden—the infamous "Singin' in the Rain" sequence. The violence of that scene got to you, forcing you to leave the theater the one and only time you tried watching with your then boyfriend. Said ex-boyfriend loved it, though...The relationship didn't last long.

"Hello?" a voice calls from downstairs. It's young, feminine. A teenage girl? "Is anyone here? I'm sorry we broke in, but we need help. My friend's hurt and someone's after us, and—"

"Up here!" you call out. "I need help too."

"Coming!" the girl shouts and then you hear footsteps bounding up the stairs. They're uneven, almost like she's limping.

You shiver, and suddenly become aware of the fact that a teenage girl is about to see you nude. "Wait!" you cry before she can come into the room.

The footfalls stop, "What is it?"

"I fell after taking a shower." You pause, trying to find the right words. "I'm not decent."

"What do you need me to do?" she asked.

"Do you see the dresser? My pajamas are in the second drawer from the top. Get me a nightgown, please."

"And underwear?" she asks, and you think about it for a moment. While you don't want your ass in the breeze while in the middle of a crisis, you don't think you can put them on without help, and you have too much pride to ask this teenage girl for said help.

"Not sure I can wear them right now. Just throw the nightgown into the room."

She does as you ask, managing to aim it so that it lands on top of you, making it easier to put on. It rides up on the side you're lying on, but it's better than giving the kid an eyeful. "Okay, I'm decent."

She pokes her head into the bathroom, and your heart stutters. She is covered in blood practically from head to foot, with a bloodied and peeling maxi pad taped to her injured arm. Judging by the way she holds her hand to her side, her ribs are either bruised or broken. Apparently, you aren't the only one having a terrible night.

"Geeze, kid, what happened to you?" you ask.

"I could ask you the same thing," she retorts as she glances around your bedroom. "Do you have a phone?"

"Yeah, it's on my nightstand." You hate how helpless you feel lying on the floor. Whatever happened to this girl, she doesn't want to talk about it, but if it followed her here, you need to know what you're up against. Not that you can fight in this condition. She looks you up and down, the mask of determination giving way to concern. "Would you like me to help you up?"

"I don't think I can walk," you reply.

"What about help you sit up?"

The idea of sitting on your broken hip is not a pleasant one, but it's better than lying down on the hard tiles, so you nod. The pain you feel when she maneuvers you to a sitting position against the bathroom cabinets is enough to make you cry out, but she covers your mouth.

"We can't make too much noise," she whispers. "He might hear."

"Who might hear?" you ask once you regain your breath after the pain of sitting up.

"We don't know," the girl replies. "We were out in the woods with some friends, and then this creep in a mask attacked us." Tears glisten in her eyes. "He killed Riley, Casey, and David. It's just me and Laurie now."

You want to take her in your arms and tell her that it will all be okay, but that would be a lie and you both will know it. You can't even stand, let alone fight off whoever is targeting these girls

"Robin, he's back," another feminine teenage voice calls out from below.

"Shit," she mutters. A part of you want to chide her for the use of language, but given the situation, a little bit of cussing feels appropriate. "Where do you keep your first aid kit?" she asks.

"I keep one in the cabinet under the sink," you reply, opening it up and pulling it out.

"I'll be right back," she says, and there's a part of you that remembers a movie from a long time ago that pointed out whoever said that particular phrase would not, in fact, be right back. But the girl, Robin, does return with her friend—Laurie, you presume—and the block of knives from your kitchen.

Laurie looks even worse off than Robin. Her skin has a grey tint and there's a massive bloody gash in her side. She's listing slightly as Robin closes the bathroom door, locks it, and shoves a towel underneath the door. When you give her a quizzical look, she shrugs and says, "If he gets in here—and he probably will, I saw him rip my friend's head off with his bare hands like it was nothing, so your door might as well be made of paper—I don't want him to see the light under the door."

You suppose that makes sense. While she treats her friend's wounds to the best of her ability, you grit your teeth against the pain and start digging through the very back of the cabinet. You know they're buried somewhere, and...aha!

There was a time when you smoked cigarettes, but that was several decades ago. When you were quitting, though, you hid this stash from your husband just in case you desperately needed a smoke. The pack and the lighter sit under a thick layer of dust, but when you test the lighter, it still works.

"Can you hand me the hairspray on top of the counter?" you ask quietly.

Robin glances up, surprised. "What for?"

"A science experiment," you reply, holding up the lighter.

She nods her approval and settles Laurie into the bathtub before pulling out your phone. "Can you call 911? I'll guard the door."

You nod and dial the number. When the almost inappropriately perky dispatcher asks about the nature of the emergency, you rush out the address and the request for police and ambulances.

"We're sending officers to your location," he says. "They're about ten minutes away."

Below, the sound of wood splitting fills the air. "Please hurry. He's coming," you whisper, turning the sound off but keeping the operator on the line. Robin, who was armed with two steak knives, hands you one, and you ready the hairspray and lighter before turning off the bathroom lights.

You both listen and wait in agonizing silence as lumbering footsteps rise up the stairs. In the darkness, with a threat looming ever closer, all you can do is wait helplessly from the floor and think about exactly how terrible this hiding spot is. The only thing between you and the killer is a flimsy door, and once he's in here, you're cornered with nowhere to run. You're as good as dead.

The floor creaks just outside the door, and you all hold your breath as the one person who can still stand readies her weapon. Something strong rams into it once, twice, three times, splintering the wood with his bare fists. She stabs the hand as it goes through the hole, impaling it. As he tries to yank it back, there's a terrible ripping sound, and his hand is partially split in half. The growl he lets out is almost inhuman.

Enraged, the murderer rips the door off its hinges, exposing you three sitting ducks. He's tall—probably six and a half feet—and broad shouldered, cutting a hulking figure. A World War I era gas mask covers his face and he's holding a rusted, bloody machete. He slashes his weapon down, nearly taking Robin's head off. She ducks out of the way at the last moment, so he only grazes her. But even though this is a decent sized bathroom, she does not have the space to move out of his reach, so with his bad hand, he grabs her by the throat and lifts her so that her feet are dangling off the ground.

You bury your kitchen knife in his thigh, praying that you severed his femoral artery and he'll bleed out when you rip it from his flesh. With a grunt, he lets her drop to the ground. Turning on the lighter and readying the hairspray, you shout, "Get clear!"

Robin dips into the glass shower stall, closing the door as you unleash the hairspray, the chemicals igniting and forming a stream of fire. The murderer screeches again, his limbs flailing about in a panic. With a battle cry, Robin rips open the door and, heedless of the flames, drives the weapon into his hulking neck. And then she does it again. And again. And again. Neck, guts, chest, limbs, and even his forehead. Then, once he's down and she's certain he's dead, she smothers the flames with a wet towel so that your house doesn't catch on fire. It's surprisingly considerate of her. You don't think you'd have the presence of mind to do that after going through a nightmare like the one she just went through.

While you wait for the police to come, you grab your knife and join in with making sure he doesn't get back up again, the pain in your hip a distant memory with all the adrenaline coursing through you. One of the first rules of those scary movies your daughter likes to watch is that you should never assume that the killer is dead. Overkill is better than underkilling, especially when you have no idea how strong or dangerous the threat is.

By the time the police and ambulance arrive, the murderer is little more than ground chuck beef from all the stab wounds. Later, after you get treatment for your broken hip, you will learn that he was an escaped serial killer who had been slicing and dicing his way through the state before stumbling upon Robin and her party.

As the police cart you out of a bathroom that is rapidly becoming more and more crowded with cops and EMTs, you decide one thing before your body gives out and you lose consciousness. Time to invest in a proper Life Alert system so that nothing like this ever happens again.

Anaphylaxis

Sheri White

Jeannette spotted the porta-potty in the clearing, grateful she wouldn't have to squat in the woods sometime during her hike. She'd been regretting the extra-large coffee she'd gotten on a whim at the Dunkin' on the way to the park.

She walked toward the structure, smelling it even from several feet away. She wrinkled her nose and grimaced, but knew she'd only be in there a short time. She avoided squatting in nature whenever possible; last time she'd gotten poison ivy in an unmentionable place and was miserable for weeks, mostly because of her boyfriend's constant snickering, but still.

She dropped her backpack against the side of the potty by the door, not wanting it to sit on the floor and get God-knows-what on it.

She closed the door, pulling it hard to keep it shut since it wouldn't latch at first, then finally slamming it and used the slide-lock. Now feeling urgency, she unbuttoned her jeans and pulled them down with her underwear, then gingerly sat on the hot plastic seat. The white-frosted roof only allowed a bit of light into the bathroom, so she blinked a few times to adjust her eyes. She heard a weird sound as she peed, but figured it was the urine stream hitting...something below her.

She finished, using the last few tissue squares left on the roll to clean up. She stood and pulled up her pants, then realized she still heard the strange sound, only louder now. She looked around, eyes now adjusted to the low light, and saw a few bees crawling on the walls.

Oh, no.

Quietly, quickly, she did up her jeans, trying to be as still as possible. Once she was finished, she unlocked the door and pushed the handle.

The door wouldn't open. She wiped her sweaty hands on her jeans and tried again, this time using both her hands and pushing on the door itself.

It wouldn't budge.

What now?

Jeannette didn't dare disturb the bees by kicking the door. She looked up again to see where the bees were, and realized there weren't just a few bees locked in with her.

There was a nest in the top corner of the tiny building. Several drips of honey coated the walls below it. Bees crawled in and out of the honeycomb.

Jeannette almost screamed before she caught herself and gasped instead. Slowly she sat back down on the plastic seat, getting as far away from the nest as she could.

She knew she was in extreme danger—not only was her phone in her backpack right outside the door, but so was her Epi Pen. Jeannette had been diagnosed with a bee allergy when she was a kid and went into anaphylactic shock after a bee stung her hand when she picked a flower. Since then, she always carried the Epi Pen in case of a sting.

Now she had no protection. But she could at least try to lessen the chance of getting stung until she could figure a way out of her predicament.

Jeannette took a ponytail holder from her wrist and braided her hair, tying it at the bottom, then tucking it up inside the baseball cap she wore. She'd had bugs get caught in her hair when hiking before, but never had to worry about a swarm of bees doing the same. She unlaced her hiking boots, took them off and removed her socks. She put the boots back on bare feet but didn't bother re-tying them yet. She put the socks on her hands, pulling them over long sleeves.

Her neck and face were still exposed, but there was nothing Jeannette could do about that except keep a sharp eye on the bees.

Okay, think. I just need to get the door open wide enough to get my backpack. Jeannette knew it wasn't an exaggeration to feel that her life depended on retrieving it if she were unable to get herself out of the porta-potty.

Jeannette was so lost in thought she didn't see the bee flying near her until she heard the buzzing by her head.

"Oh, shit!" she whispered loudly. Instinctively she used a sock-covered hand to swat it away. The bee hit the wall with a satisfying THWACK, dying instantly.

Jeannette put her face in her hands, breathing rapidly and hoping they weren't the kind of bees that got pissed off and attacked when one was killed.

The buzzing got a little louder; however, the bees didn't swarm her and sting.

But now more were crawling on the walls, getting closer to her. Jeannette used her hands to brace against the plastic seat and lowered herself to the piss-sticky floor. She wouldn't let herself think about what else she was sitting on. She put her forehead on her knees and wrapped her arms around the back of her neck to cover herself as much as possible. As long as the bees were only crawling on the walls and not flying around her, she would be okay.

She knew she couldn't stay that way for a long time, but had no choice until she figured a way to get out of the building.

She raised her head and chuckled a bit. "This is ridiculous! I'm stuck in a disgusting porta-potty with a fucking bees' nest! I could die with my head next to a trough filled with piss and shit. It's completely ludicrous."

Jeannette pushed her foot against the door, testing to see if the bottom had more give to it. A tiny bit of sunlight peeked through a crack between the door and front of the structure. Her heart leapt a bit at the sight.

I can do this. I can get out of here.

***

Jeannette worked at pushing the door with her foot for what seemed like hours. Sweat dripped down her face, and trickled from her breasts and armpits inside her clothes. She wiped the sweat from her face with her sock-covered hands, which were now soaked through.

She had made progress, though. The door was giving more, but the unavoidable noise had agitated the bees, and more flew around her. A couple crawled on her jeans, and she swatted them away like she had the one before. This time, the killer bees did attract more ticked-off bees, and Jeannette knew she had to move fast before even just one stung her.

She almost broke the seal on the plastic door when it made a loud CRACK, and bees angrily swarmed her. Quickly she took the socks off her hands and placed them on the back of her neck, then shoved her hands into the front of her shirt. With just a second's hesitation, she turned around and put her feet against the plastic trough and shoved against it so her back pushed on the door.

The bottom half of the door opened several inches. Encouraged, Jeannette did it several more times, harder each time, until the door finally gave way, spilling her out of the porta-potty onto her back. She let out of sob of relief and began to sit up but didn't get the chance before the bees were on her.

Her arms inside her shirt pushed the shirt up, exposing her stomach, and the bees immediately swarmed this bit of flesh. Dozens stung her, making her scream in pain and terror. She pulled her arms out of the shirt to brush them off, but others now stung those areas as well. She felt a bee crawling on her face and swatted it away.

Anaphylactic shock began to set in. Angry red hives raised up on Jeannette's skin. She felt like vomiting, but her throat was closing up and her breathing began to slow.

She knew she was dying.

With much effort, she moved her left hand around in the grass, searching for her backpack. She found it and was able to grab her Epi Pen from the side pocket.

She had no strength to jab it into her leg, though. Jeannette kept pushing the Epi Pen at her leg, but she couldn't get the needle to penetrate her thigh muscle.

Her breathing grew more shallow and slow, and the Epi Pen rolled from her hand as she lost consciousness.

***

Months later, a group of hikers stumbled upon the scene. A couple of them screamed in horror.

Dead bees surrounded Jeannette's body. Most of her skin had decomposed. The open porta-potty was now filled with bees and honeycomb. The buzzing of thousands of honeybees drowned out any nearby normal sounds like birds and crickets.

Bees crawled in and out of Jeannette's mouth. Her eyes were gone, and the sockets were filled with honey, oozing out the side into the grass, like thick amber tears.

The four hikers stood and gaped at the horrific sight for a few moments, until one of them urged the others to get moving.

"Come on," said Jimmy. "Let's go get a ranger or something."

"Good idea," answered Matt. "I'm allergic anyway, so let's get far away from those things."

Intervention

Matthew Hall

Before excusing himself from the table, Marley's hands had begun to shake. Winston hadn't noticed, until Marley nearly spilled his drink. That's when he excused himself. A tell-tale sign, Winston thought. He was already suspicious of his friend's habits, but had yet to confirm his suspicions.

How would he do it? Would he march into the washroom and confront his friend? Winston asked himself how someone like Marley, who was so shy he sometimes stammered, could perform such an intimate ritual in such a public place (not just any washroom, but a washroom in a Burger King, of all places!). And then he asked himself how long he would wait before intervening (long enough for Marley to let his guard down, he decided).

When the time came, Winston held his breath, opened the door slowly, and crept in - trying to enter the washroom without making any noise that might alert Marley. Not that it would have made any difference. Marley was locked in one of the stalls, the only occupied stall, and from the sound of things he must be too preoccupied to notice anyone coming or going.

Winston heard the lighter - it must have been nearly empty, because he heard Marley struggling with the spark wheel. He could have interrupted then, but instead he waited - waited until he heard the tap tap of Marley's fingernail flicking the syringe - before knocking.

"Marley," he shouted, between knocks. "You in there?"

Winston heard the clatter of something metallic hitting the floor. The sound, amplified by the reverberant tiles, made it seem like a large object had been dropped. But when Winston looked down, all he saw was a spoon, and a small one at that.

"Marley?"

"Just a minute," came a timid voice from inside the stall. Winston barely recognized it as Marley's voice.

He knocked again.

"Come out, Marley," he said, "or I'm coming in."

"Wait! Please!"

Winston gave up knocking. He tried something that he'd seen in a cop drama - he shook the door until he heard something come loose. He hadn't expected it to work, but he was glad it had - he had an aversion to public washrooms in general, and dreaded the prospect of lowering himself onto the grimy floor and crawling under the partition, knowing that he wasn't physically fit enough to climb over.

The door swung open and there was Marley - his sleeve rolled up, arm tied, and a syringe held in his opposite hand, hovering impatiently above a network of track marks.

"Marley," he said. "What are you doing?"

He knew it was a foolish thing to say. He already suspected what Marley was doing, he wouldn't have come into the washroom otherwise, and now that he'd caught him in the act it was more obvious than before. But, unprepared for the sight of his friend in such a compromising position, he was short of words.

"It's not what you think," Marley said. "If you trust me, you'll let me do this!"

"How am I supposed to trust you?"

"I'm trying to tell you," Marley said. "This isn't what it looks like!"

"It looks like you're, uh, shooting up."

Marley nodded his head reluctantly. He said, "Yes, technically I am. But it's not what you think it is."

"What?" Winston asked. Without knowing what Winston was thinking, Marley had said that it wasn't what Winston thought - three times, no less! It raised his guard. He thought of all the books he'd read and movies he'd watched involving addicts - they were always portrayed as desperate, manipulative, and ruthless; quick to lie, cheat, or . . . whatever necessary to secure their next fix. The question was, what kind of manipulation was this?

Before Winston could answer his own question, he felt the ground shift beneath his feet. The tiles remained solid, but it was as if the foundation itself had been replaced by something unstable, causing the tiles to separate from each other and sag under his weight. Marley must have felt it too, because he lost his balance and fell off the toilet.

The syringe fell with a clink onto the floor. Marley reached for it, but the ground shifted - not under anyone's or anything's weight, but as if it had a mind of its own - causing the syringe to roll away.

Marley tried to climb under the partition and into the next stall, following the syringe, but he wasn't halfway across when the ground beneath him raised up - pinning Marley to the partition. Marley cried out in pain. To Winston he looked like an insect between the giant fingers of the room itself.

My God, Winston thought, he'll be crushed to death!

He took hold of Marley's legs, tried to pull him back the way he came, but it was no good. He rushed out of the stall, thinking he'd have better luck pulling Marley's upper half, and immediately fell - having yet to adjust to the malleable floor. *I'm better off crawling*, he decided, and consciously slowed his breathing in an effort to overcome the panic he felt - panic so intense that he didn't give a second thought to crawling on the floor of a public washroom that he would have otherwise found disgusting.

When he crawled into the next stall, Winston found Marley writhing under the partition. Although the ground was malleable in other places, it was rigid beneath Marley. And the partition appeared to be pressing down on his back like a guillotine. Marley writhed and moaned. He didn't notice anyone had entered the stall, until Winston said, "What's happening?"

"I was - I was trying to tell you," Marley said, between moans. "There's some kind of - some kind of curse on me."

"Did you say curse?"

"It's a - a long story," Marley said. "The only way to stop - to stop the curse is with - is with an herb. I don't - I don't like to inject it, but - but it's the fastest way."

"Take it easy, you can tell me later," Winston said, hoping there would be a later. "I'm sorry I thought you were . . ."

"I know, I know," Marley said. "It's okay! Just please just - just go find it so I can - so I can take my shot."

"We've got to get you out of here first!"

Winston reached for Marley, but Marley pushed his hands away - awkwardly, because of the contorted posture he had assumed under the partition.

"There's no time," Marley said. "Go! And be careful!"

Winston knew which way to go, but he wouldn't make the same mistake as Marley. He crawled out of the second stall, feeling the tiles sink under his hands and knees, and into the third stall, where he knew the syringe awaited him - it had come to rest at the base of the toilet.

He picked up the syringe and slipped it into his breast pocket, then looked around, expecting something to jump out at him or otherwise threaten him. But nothing came. It can't be this easy, Winston thought. Can it?

When he crawled out of the stall, his disbelief was confirmed - it was confirmed again and again and again by the stalls that had proliferated while he was in the third stall. The room had become infinitely large, and there were stalls as far as his eyes could see.

Winston felt the air leave his lungs, and struggled to fill them again. On the verge of hyperventilating, he raised the collar of his shirt over his head and breathed into it - like the paper bags he used when he was a kid.

After he'd composed himself, he shouted, "Marley?"

He waited for an answer.

Nothing.

He shouted again, "Marley?"

He waited.

Nothing.

Louder this time, "Marley!"

This time he heard a faint voice in the distance.

He started crawling toward it, but sensed that the environment was growing more unstable - his hands and knees were sinking deeper and deeper into the tile, the light flickering and threatening to plunge him into darkness . . .

Winston grappled with a sense of urgency and a sense of futility. One option presented itself, but he resisted the option. He crawled and crawled, resisting the temptation of that option - the one and only? - until he succumbed to the belief that he wasn't making progress, and the sense of futility overcame him.

The ground seemed to level then. The room was no longer conspiring against him. Winston rolled up his sleeve. He took off his belt, put the tongue through the look, and pulled it tight around his arm. The syringe was at the ready in his pocket.

This was it. His one and only option.

***

When he regained consciousness, Winston saw Marley kneeling above him. His face was creased with concern, but sweet relief smoothed those creases when Winston sat up.

But sitting up caused Winston to wince. The belt was still fastened tight. He loosened it, but he didn't have the strength to sow it through the loops in his pants.

Marley reached for Winston. At first he thought Marley was reaching for the belt, but instead Marley gripped his arm, turning it around so both men could see the hole from the injection.

"You shouldn't have done that," Marley said

"It was the only way."

"I know," Marley said. "But you still shouldn't have done that."

"Why?"

"How d'you think I got the curse?"

Winston hadn't thought about it, hadn't had time to think about it, but that was all he needed to hear to know how Marley had gotten it, and how he'd shared it with Winston.

It Lives Within

Nico Bell

Asher fumbled with the lock of the bathroom stall, finally managing to slide it into place. It wouldn't do much, but with Mia slowly walking along the stalls, stalking her prey with malicious glee, pushing in the doors open one-by-one, the tiny piece of metal was the only thing standing between her and yet another beat down.

"Come out, freak." Mia's voice held a familiar taunt.

They'd been friends once, before Mia's breasts filled out her bra and Asher started tapping theirs flat to their chest. Things were less complicated back when friendship meant knotted bracelets and daisy chain necklaces. As soon as they hit high school and Asher knew they weren't like the other kids in the school, friendship evolved into taking a stand, sticking up for each other, and that's where Mia faltered.

Really, it should be Asher stalking Mia in the girl's bathroom. Their anger flared, but they quickly squelched it with a bitter swallow. No, they couldn't blame Mia for siding with the cool kids. She was doing the same thing as Asher: trying to survive.

An airy giggle echoed against the tiled floor and sent a shiver through Asher. Mia wasn't alone. Of course not. Asher held her breath as they looked through the crack between the door and the stall's wall. A flash of red hair caused them to gasp as they stumbled backwards until the back of their knees hit the toilet seat.

Not Sophie. Anyone but her.

The scar on her forearm burned in memory of their last encounter.

"Please," they hated the way their voice cracked and the desperation dripping from the single plea. Somewhere, buried deep within, a strong version of themselves lived; someone people didn't push around; someone able to fight. Every now-and-then, when they laid in their bed long after their mother came home from her second shift at the restaurant and her exhausted snores filled the small space between their two tiny bedrooms, they looked up at the dark ceiling and felt it. A stir. Something visceral and demanding. A twinge that burned with passion and power. A knowledge that they were worthy of life and living. And even though the feeling always disappeared by morning, buried under insecurities and a chest binder, it comforted Asher to know it lurked deep within.

If only that part of themself would rise up, but it remained dormant and still, buried under piles of fear.

The bathroom door rattled as Sophie pushed against it. "Mia, get over here and help me open this."

Asher silently willed Mia to remember all the late night texting sessions, the pizza and movie nights, the sleepovers filled with silly games and laughter. They wanted to ask if Mia still had the little stuffed zebra they had bought her as a souvenir during their fourth grade field trip to the zoo and if maybe, just this one, she could tap back into her old self and remember that Asher wasn't a freak. Asher was still the same person that painted her nails electric banana yellow and taught her how to French braid her hair. Instead, they cringed as the two girls pounded on the bathroom stall, laughing as their firsts rattled the door.

"Stop, please. Just leave me alone." Asher squeezed their eyes shut and covered their ears, the two girls' taunting still ringing through their body as the voices outside the stall grew louder, hurling insults and threats. Heat stirred beneath their skin, flaming from their core, and sweeping over their nerves. Pain erupted and they clenched their fists, digging their nails into the palms of their hands, trying to focus on anything other than the panic and fear overtaking their senses.

Something stirred within. They clutched their stomach. Dizziness distorted their vision, spinning the bathroom stall around until they dropped to their knees and hurled into the toilet.

Then, everything stopped. The heat, the pain, and even the taunting all ended abruptly.

Asher wiped the sweat from her brow and, on shaky knees, stood to face the bathroom door. Beneath the gap, Mia and Sophie's feet had turned and were pointed as if the girls now faced the back of the room.

"Where'd you come from?" Sophie's voice held an emotion Asher had never heard come out of the bully's mouth: fear.

The school bell rang, signaling the need to hurry to class. Asher jumped at the sound.

"We should go," Mia's voice waivered.

"Hey, I asked you a question." Sophie's old confidence began to bloom in tone. "Who are you? Another freak? What's wrong with you, huh? Why do you look like that?"

"Sophie, we need to leave."

Asher watched Mia's shoes step away from the stall, but Sophie's remained rooted in place.

"Fine. Stay if you want, but I'm out of here." The bathroom door creaked, the sounds of chatter and movement from the hall filled the tense silence, and then, the door closed, muffling the outside world once again.

"What are you doing? Stay away from me."

Asher's breath held tight in their chest as a crash rang out from the other side of the closed door. A scream quickly snuffed to silence, and beneath the bathroom door, Sophie's body sprawled on the tiles.

"It's safe for you to come out now," a voice with a very familiar tone spoke.

Asher's hands trembled and hoovered over the lock.

"Seriously, it's okay. Come out and see. You won't get hurt."

Asher believed the person with startling certainty. They knew they shouldn't unlatch the lock. They knew it would be smarter to stay locked away until someone came to their rescue, but who? Even if a student came into the bathroom at that exact moment, what would she see? Sophie, on the floor, maybe unconscious or worse. Then, it would only be a matter of seconds before a teacher got involved, then the principal, and maybe even the cops.

Would anyone believe they were the true victim? No. Mia would be the witness and weave some sort of lie painting a new reality where Asher instigated everything. She'd done it before.

With nothing to lose, Asher opened the bathroom stall door. Sophie laid on her back, gasping and clutching her side where long scratches tore through her shirt and broke her flesh. Blood stained the floor, but Asher sensed it wasn't as bad as it looked. It certainly wasn't as bad as what Sophie had done to them. Standing to the side was a creature mirroring Asher's height and weight, but that's where the similarities ended. The creature's skin illuminated in the halogen lights, radiant and sparkling. Asher squinted against the glow. It didn't wear clothing, but there was no discernable anatomy as to gender, just an outline of a being with no hair, dark round eyes, and a thin mouth. It stood on long legs and the arms hung to its side. Asher noticed the blood dripping from the tips of its sharp fingernails.

It was beautiful.

"Help me."

Asher completely forgot about Sophie, and anger flared at her plea's interruption of this moment. Suddenly, Asher felt more vulnerable than ever. A protective desire to shield the creature from Sophie grew stronger with each passing second, and they stepped up to Sophie and kneeled, ignoring the scent of sweat and blood.

"You have to go get someone. Please. It hurts." Sophie's tears slid down her cheeks. The creature bent down also so that their face rested mere centimeters from the bully's. Sophie whimpered and tried to wiggle away, but she squeaked in pain and remained still.

The creature's tongue lashed out and slurped up the tears. It looked to Asher and smiled.

Asher smiled back.

It reached out its hand and Asher didn't hesitate. They let their fingertips trace its fingers and wrist, gently slipping their palm into its so they held hands as they stood. Sophie continued to whimper.

"Who are you?" But Asher knew. Deep down, the answer resided within. Somehow, they'd conjured this being into existence just when they needed it most. And now that it was released, Asher knew it could never again be contained.

"I'll never bother you again. I swear," Sophie pleaded. "I won't tell anyone what really happened here, okay?"

"No," Asher and the creature spoke in unison. "You need to tell all the other people you hang out with. Mia, especially. Make sure everyone knows exactly what you did, and make sure they know that anyone who tries to do the same will get a similar punishment."

The creature smirked. "Or worse."

Sophie nodded. "Whatever you want."

"Get up."

Sophie winced but managed to rise. She held her wound and hurried to the door. Giving one last look, she stared at Asher and then the creature, then she bolted into the hallway.

They knew they should feel some sort of regret for hurting Sophie, maybe even fear of retaliation, but Asher relaxed. Their hand in the creature's calmed any rising concerns. It didn't matter what happened next. It didn't matter who tried to hurt them in the future.

Asher was ready, and she would survive.

Trimmings

Kassidy VanGundy

"Next, you are just going to want to come around from the back and bring the clippers forward..."

Melissa obediently does what she is told, taking these video instructions from one of YouTube's most popular hairdressers as gospel. After all, his perfect blonde highlights speak for themselves.

"Good! Once you have your first streak going, feel free to start again in the opposite direction..."

She follows suit, drowning any thoughts of dissent with the buzzing of her electric razor and allowing strands of her dark brown hair to fall casually into her sink.

After a couple of months of quarantine, Melissa needs a drastic change in her increasingly monotonous life. She's become stir crazy. Trapped in her tiny studio apartment with nothing but her own thoughts, Melissa stares into the mirror for the first time without any distractions and is forced to confront what she sees. Her lengthening hair continues to blind her, getting in the way of her vision and preventing her from making any actual progress in life. Since no one is going to see her in person anyway, if there is any time in her life where Melissa would shave her head, she figures it would be now.

"Great! Soon your head should be perfectly buzzed! If you want to take it a step further, feel free to click on the next video where I teach you how to finish off the look with a Gillette razor -"

Melissa taps the pause button on her phone. She stares down at it for a good while, trying to decide between going completely bald, or mixing a bunch of leftover hair dye in the cabinet together and dumping it on her head. Truthfully, the hair dye is probably expired, considering she bought it during an impromptu trip to Sally's Beauty Supply with her best friend when her ex dumped her pre-pandemic. How many months ago was that? An entire year?! It seems like a lifetime ago anyway.

She decides that this wouldn't be the best time to be rushed to the hospital for a chemical burn or an extreme allergic reaction, so bald it is. Grabbing the pink comfort glide razor from the edge of her tub, Melissa prepares herself to take this leap. She presses the play button on her touch screen once more, letting the hairdresser's voice hypnotize her once more during this drastic transformation.

"Welcome back to another video on my channel!! Today we're doing a complete shave on my good friend..."

***

After the most meticulous hour of her life, Melissa finishes her head shave with a handful of minor cuts and scrapes. Basking in the glory of her freshly shaved head, Melissa runs her fingers over her pale skin, taking in the unfamiliar slippery texture left behind by the use of strawberry shaving cream. Blood inevitably mixes in with this sticky consistency, giving Melissa quite the fright when she spots these globs of red in the knobs of her head for the first time. She looks around for her first aid kit in the medicine cabinet, hoping to find some much needed Band-Aids.

However, something else catches her attention.

A matted, dark brown thing squirms about in the dark crevices of the sink, popping out of the shadows every now and then to reel in bits of her dry cut hair and pull them further down into the drain. She can't make out a distinctive shape, but panics anyway, her brain filling in the blanks with its own preconceived notions. It must be a rat of some sort looking for materials to build a nest.

Fearing the worst, Melissa rushes to turn the handle of the sink, unleashing a stream of hot water onto whatever critter could be scurrying about in the pipe. She hopes this would be enough to deter it from emerging, that it would simply go back to wherever it came from and never be seen again. As a side effect, the remnants of her DIY haircut also get swept up in the torrent, following the home intruder back down into the sewer.

After a few minutes of letting the water flow, Melissa finally feels comfortable enough to turn the knob and shut it off. Shivers travel up and down her spine at the thought of having rodents in the apartment again, especially since she couldn't rely on a partner to get rid of them for her anymore. She would have to call the maintenance man in the morning, but for now, the best thing she can do is get a nice warm shower to wash off any germs she could have picked up from this encounter.

Melissa turns around and reaches for the shower handle, but is interrupted once more by an unwanted guest making its way out of her pipes.

A hand, a slimy, furry hand crawls its way upward from the shower drain. She watches helplessly as the woolly fingers squeeze their way out of the holes of the duct, looking for a way to unscrew the metal guard altogether. They continue to grow in size, spreading their influence all over the bottom of the tub.

Melissa frantically reaches for the Drano under the sink, hoping that this would be enough to keep whatever this is at bay. An ear piercing shrill emanates from the fur as Melissa dumps the cleaning chemicals all over it indiscriminately. The hair constituting the digits of the hand start to erode away, causing the hand to recoil even further into the drain. Melissa begins to celebrate internally as the smell of burning hair floods the airspace within the cramped bathroom.

However, very quickly these fumes get the best of her, causing Melissa to grow dizzier and dizzier by the second. In between blacked out spots in her vision, Melissa searches for the small bathroom window next to the toilet and tries to pry it open for some fresh air. Using what strength she has left, Melissa manages to crack open the window slightly, just enough for a slight breeze to roll in. She takes in a deep breath and exhales, ridding herself of the toxicity in the room once and for all. Melissa lets the oddly soothing city air linger in her lungs, taking a split second to recenter herself after everything that's passed.

Little did she know this would be her last brief moment of peace.

***

The gradual crescendo of creaking pipes pulls Melissa away from the window. She turns her head slowly and looks over her shoulder to see rivers of disgusting wet hair pour out of every crevice in the bathroom: the sink, the shower head and drain, and the toilet as well. They all congregate in the center of the room, where they build on top of one another until a solid mass forms. With her back pinned against the wall, Melissa watches as the mound of discarded hair grows even taller, increasing in size until it finally towers over her.

And there it is, the amalgamation of every poor life decision she's ever made all at once, standing directly before her. Rainbow clumps of vibrantly dyed matted hair signifying every breakup she's ever had, and the significant "glow up" that would follow. The trimmings of shaved legs in preparation for every date she ended up canceling. The leftover strands of her visitors, romantic or otherwise, that would cleanse themselves of her presence right before they had to leave. They all inevitably had to leave.

Melissa stares at this personification of regret, this humanoid ball of hair right in its blank face. Some of its coat pulls away from itself, revealing a deeper void within the monster.

A hole forms in the middle of its head, giving it the ability to speak.

"Feeeeeeeed meeeeeeeee..."

The creature lifts one of its arms in a clumsy fashion and drops it down onto her shoulder, causing Melissa to shiver at the unsavory texture of its wet pelt. However, this disgust would be short-lived. A sharp pain takes over as the overgrown mane of the creature uses the strands of its own hair to pluck her peach fuzz off of her skin, leaving behind inflamed strawberry bumps in its wake.

She tries to let out a scream, but the monster uses its other soaked hand to cover her mouth, muffling her for good.

"Feeeeeeeed meeeeeeeeee..."

Melissa can feel the bulky hand of the monster rob her of her blonde mustache hairs, the ones she feverishly denied were there in the first place. It spreads out, grabbing bunches of her baby hairs from her face and claiming them for itself. Satisfied moans leak from the mouth of the monster with every minute strand of hair it consumes.

Soon the hairy monster makes his way upward, painfully yanking out her eyelashes one by one. Her eyes water in response, but the creature does not care. It just as easily moves onto its next victim: the eyebrows she intentionally kept bushy to keep up with her "clean girl" aesthetic. They are her pride and joy, and prove to be a very fulfilling meal for the giant hairball now covering nearly every inch of her skin.

When they are finally through with her face, both arms of the creature glide up to the top of her head, where they now find a barren food desert. Sniffing around out of desperation, the monster's hide nearly burrows itself into her skin. They try to scoop out whatever they can from her hair follicles, like plucking oysters out of their shells. The tips of their soaked hair stings like knives, causing tears to flood down Melissa's face.

"Noooooo mmmooooorrreeeee fffoooooooood?"

The creature screams out in pure agony.

Pushing past the throbbing pain, Melissa tries her best to turn her head, to break away from the tight grip of the creature. This only angers the monster even further, causing it to violently screech in her face. Tiny droplets of sewer water spray from its mouth and land onto her bare face. Melissa winces as it spreads its fur down to her throat like a network of small ropes, encircling her neck over and over again. With every iteration, the raging mane squeezes her throat tighter and tighter, choking her with her own discarded hair. Melissa starts seeing spots once again, as the monster cuts off her airway, blocking any oxygen from reaching her brain. However, in between these gaps in her sight, Melissa swears she can see the face of her ex in the outline of the monster, faintly, just faintly, but this thought is fleeting. It doesn't matter much in the grand scheme of things anyway, especially now as Melissa is being carried off by the still blackness of eternal night.

Voices and Reflections

Christine LaChance

Collect. Retrieve. Enfold yourself.

You are one.

Three...two...one.

There were too many of him. He knew it wasn't right. There could be only one. There *should* be only one. He only needed a moment alone, a moment to breathe, knowing it would always be a fight. Guiding his will, breaking the surface of the brewing tide of chaos inside his mind and soul, he pulled himself, all of himself together. This time had been far too close.

Taking a moment, feeling all of himself put in its proper place, he prepared himself to meet his reflection. He would be there, he just wasn't sure which, and how many, *hes* would be looking back at him. There should only be one. There had to be only one, otherwise, he would be trapped in this psychiatric ward forever. He dared to open his eyes, confident he had closed the doors within. For the first time in months, he had a chance to look at himself. Meeting the gaze of the man in the mirror, alone at last, he could see only himself in front of empty stalls. The sight was always unsettling. The man looking back at him was barely recognizable, but the reflection moved with him. He was the one there. He had grown pale over these many months. The yellow light of the bathroom cast a sickly yellow over him, adding to the sickliness of his gaunt appearance. The clothing the ward provided him, hung loosely over his nearly skeletal body. Not a smile, or even the hint of happiness touched his miserable face. The dark circles around his eyes had grown wider. He was fading, so very thin now. He held up a bony hand to his reflection and flexed his fingers. The reflection did the same, almost saying hello. "Hello, me. Been a while. Are we alone?" Yes. One. He was one.

Outside, the nurse waited to bring him back to his room for his medication. The doctor had decided to lighten up the dosage, to see how he would stand without the crutch that had been holding him in a fog all these months. He had to be quick in here, before she suspected something was wrong. He had been doing so well, well enough that the doctor granted him small liberties, and the nurses began to trust him for short spans of time on his own. He was taking advantage of such luxuries now, a little time alone. The doctor couldn't know about this regression, this unfortunate relapse. He knew he would lose everything. He'd be back on those meds, lost in a trance of numbness. "Count your blessings," he told his reflection. "You got away from that nurse in time. You may have saved a life." He had feigned sickness, an immediate need to vomit. The nurse had believed him. The doctor had been slowly weaning him off of his daily cocktail of medications, and the effects of withdrawal were to be expected. The nurse would never know the danger she was suddenly in when he felt the familiar shift. He had to control it himself. He finally knew how. It was time for him to take charge. Now, out of the drug fog, beginning to feel like a person again, he could truly begin his healing.

This had been a problem for as long as he could remember. There was a darkness within he couldn't ignore, but he could control, a voice that called deep from within. It told him things. It forced him. The years went by, and the voice became louder, took control. He had been helpless against it. This was the problem. He had to accept he had been a bad kid, who grew into a bad man, a man who had done terrible things.

A splash of water on the face would settle his nerves, a cleanse. "Think logically. These are just your aspects. They are you," he reminded himself. "Don't fear them. Control them." This is what the doctor had assured him in their many, many sessions together. "We all have them. We filter. We don't allow them to control us. You have to learn how to do this. Some of your aspects have been allowed too much freedom. That, I believe, is the source of your problem." The good doctor believed he could be treated with a series of therapy sessions, and drugs, so many drugs. The months had faded away like a mist on the sea. The numbness, the near catatonic state he had been left in, left no room for a relapse, no opportunity for the darkness to arise. It was better than the prison sentence he would have faced, he supposed, but was this in a way, not also a prison? He was watched, controlled, even with all this progress.

It was still there, just below the surface. He could feel it practically scraping at his skull, poking at his eyes to be let out. He held his thin fingers under the rushing water from the metallic faucet, waiting for it to go cold enough to chill his warm face, to bring him back to where his body stood. Water, so holy and cooling.

Maybe he should have worked with that priest after all. He also saw another presence within. "You don't need drugs and therapy, my son. You need cleansing. The more time that passes, the stronger it will get. Don't lose yourself to evil. Don't let it take you."

His throat tightened, remembering what the priest had said. No, it wasn't possible he was possessed. He was the evil one, a bad seed. He had done those terrible things. The doctor had reminded him of this every day. There was no blaming his terrible deeds on something he had done himself.

He felt his stomach twist into a heavy knot. The very idea of anything other than himself within his body filled him with pure dread. There was no way. It wasn't possible. He was just a bad man. The evidence proved this.

Not waiting for the water to cool further, he cupped his hands, and splashed icy water on his face and over his head. He felt hot. It had been quite a battle. "Breathe," he whispered to himself. "Close the gates, seal the cages. It's gone."

"*Gone?*"

That voice. The voice he heard in his waking nightmares. The voice he carried with him since he was a child. His closing didn't work. It was okay. The voice was quiet. Even if he was heating up again, he could handle this.

"*You can't keep ignoring me. You know this.*"

He knew it was right, but he wouldn't allow this. "Leave me alone. You don't belong out here." He whispered to his reflection, not wanting to attract the attention of the nurse waiting for him on the other side of the door.

The voice let out a chuckle. "*Don't belong? I've been with you all these years.*" The words had come out of his own mouth. The lips of his reflection began to scowl.

"You are a part of who I am. You aren't welcome on the outside. Something like you belongs behind closed doors." His reflection was beginning to unnerve him. The man before him was deteriorating, and he hated it. He couldn't deny it. Even with the understanding, he wasn't him anymore. He was a sickly patient on the verge of breaking.

"*They're trying to destroy you. Look at what they've done.*" The snarling man in the mirror was fading. He was no longer what he once was. "*I can save us.*"

He thrust a stunned look up at his gaunt reflection. "Save us? There is no us. There is me. I will save myself by containing you once and for all."

His reflection smiled menacingly at him. "*Yes. There is only me. You've made me a part of you. You will never be rid of me now. Don't deny me.*"

He gripped tightly to the sink, feeling the heat overwhelm him. He was weak, far too faded from what he once was to keep the doors closed. Who even was he now? "I don't want this anymore."

The reflection snarled, face contorted into an image of pure hatred. "*Then don't fight me!*" He leaned back his head, then thrust it into the mirror. His reflection became trapped in the spider web pattern of the impact and pieces of broken glass shattered into the porcelain sink before him. The light around him began to fade. Shadows were thrown from his very essence. Before him, the mirror cracked. Darkness surrounded him for a moment. Looking back at the broken mirror, deep within the web of cracks, a man stood tall, healthy, even if he was a little pale. He looked well-rested and confident in himself. The therapy, the drugs, they had really been doing wonders for him. The false image the voice had projected on him had finally done its work and he was able to stop seeing himself as such a broken man, fighting an impossible battle. There was nothing wrong. Now that control had been restored, all would be well. *"Rest now. I'm in control."*

The bathroom door opened just enough for the nurse to look inside. "What happened? I heard some glass break."

He turned and smiled at the startled woman. "My apologies. I slipped on some water and caught the mirror."

The nurse narrowed her eyebrows at his words. "You sound a bit different. Does your throat hurt?"

He let out a chuckle. "I feel more myself than I have in months, *nurse.*"

She returned the smile. "Wonderful. The doctor will be thrilled."

He tactfully leaned over the sink, feigning a sudden head injury. The shards of mirror were ripe for harvesting in that sink. Quickly, he scooped up a shard large enough to do the dark deed he needed to commit. He hid a shard of broken mirror in his hand as he beckoned the woman to come closer. "Nurse," he lied, "I might have hit my head harder than I thought. Would you mind taking a look?"

Silver Fish

Hughes Ouimet

Trista was looking at her reflection in a razor blade. Standing at her bathroom mirror, she wondered how much pressure it would take to end it all. The problem was the lack of courage. She felt like a coward. *Not today,* she thought before setting the blade back on the side of the sink. Always in plain sight, as a reminder that it was always an option.

Three months ago, Brad had left her. No second chance, no hopes. His stuff was already moved when she came home to their overpriced three-bedroom apartment on one famous evening. Words were that he already had someone new. Maybe he had an affair. All he left her was a note saying, "Sorry, it's over..." and a month's rent paid. She spent that month crying and looking for a new home. Avoiding people as much as she could. She was never the social type anyway. Probably one of her flaws as a girlfriend.

The next month after that she spent it in her new, much cheaper, loft apartment. It was located in a basement that reeked of humidity. The perfect place to be depressed one would think. At least she had her own bathroom, and she was all alone in her sorrow. She kept family and friends at bay. She wouldn't respond to any texts and all her phone calls were going directly into voicemail.

When someone would drop by to make sure she was still alive and tell her that maybe, just maybe, she could seek help, she would step outside the door and make excuses. Sometimes she would only let them see a shadow underneath the door so they would know she was alive. She would then yell something like, "I'm fine! Please, I just want to be alone! Don't worry about me, I'll come around!". The thing was that she wasn't fine, and she wasn't about to come around anytime soon. She spent her days sleeping to The Big Bang Theory menu playing on a loop in the background and feeding on ramen almost daily, not bothering cooking them anymore. These days and generations felt ideal for her. Everything was a text or a phone call away. Groceries, food or anything were delivered right to your doorstep. No need to see anybody. It was exactly what she wanted. Exactly what she thought she needed. It was also her worst enemy.

Somehow her bathroom was the only place she felt somewhat sane. It was a tiny private space. A bath on one side, a toilet in the middle facing a countertop sink and on the other side a washer and dryer she hadn't used yet. The bathroom was acting like a sort of no man's land between her world and the outside. There were no expectations. It was timeless. Trista wasn't working. Her hygiene was degrading fast. All she wanted was to sleep and not exist for as long as she possibly could. So, every day when she spotted that blade, the idea was very appealing. But not today.

What the hell? she thought as she saw movement beside her on the floor. She looked just in time to see a tiny bug crawling under the gray carpet in front of the bathtub. When she lifted the carpet, not one but three bugs went crawling in every direction, looking to hide in any darkness they could find. Disgusted, she quickly armed herself with a piece of toilet paper. One of the bugs quickly squeezed its elastic body under the baseboard while another managed to hide in a darkened crack of the tiled floor, impossible for Trista to locate. The third bug wasn't so lucky. It was just standing there in the middle of a floor tile, either playing dead or watching Trista's next move. She quickly squished the bug. Then she lifted the paper to have a look at the damage. The bug had left a trace of silver on the floor and on the paper. Its body almost exterminated under the pressure. *Gross motherfucker!* she thought. Without paying it any more attention, she flushed the paper and was making her way back to her room when she felt a trembling sensation. The walls, the washer and dryer, the shower curtain, everything started to shake. Even the razor blade fell into the sink. It made a clinking noise, like a notification, reminding her that the possibility was always there. Bracing herself on the door jamb, she wondered, *is that a fucking earthquake? Please let this building fall on me and those stupid bugs and end it!* The quake ended as if it had heard her. Trista felt deceived. She started sobbing in despair as she slowly made her way back to her bed to sleep.

The next week kept its routine. The staring at the blade and the crushing of bugs. According to the internet, they were called Silverfish. Most surprisingly were the more frequent earthquakes. Maybe only twice in her life had she witnessed an earthquake and she always lived in the neighborhood. As crazy as it sounded, it seemed to her that every time she squished one of those bugs, there was an earthquake. Sometimes very strong, some barely noticeable. This led her to think for the first time that she was losing her damn mind. Maybe she needed to go out, see the world, get out of her dungeon of anxiety. The truth was that only the thought of it was making her feel nauseated. So, she would retreat even deeper into oblivion.

The sighting of bugs kept coming. Always in the bathroom. Their sizes are always varying but growing. She even saw one munching on a piece of chip that had accumulated its fair amount of dust on the floor. *These little fuckers even eat our food?* she thought. Every time she would lift the carpet or the overflowing trash, a few would run around. She would squish as many as she could. She would even use the sole of her socks, before throwing them in the also overflowing washer. At night, on the rare occasions she was not sleeping, she felt she could hear them in the bathroom and in the walls. Hell, she probably had some underneath her bed. *What about my blankets?* she feared. Her body was itching from head to toe, as if she could feel them crawling on her skin. When she would find sleep again, she would dream about them.

One night, while grabbing a glass of water, and at the same time always keeping an eye on that damn blade, she noticed something odd. In the darkness of the bathroom, through the reflection of the mirror, she noticed that the corner of the wall on top of the bath was oddly darker than the rest. *A trick of shadows perhaps?* she thought. Only it was moving. She slowly turned around to have a better look.

"What the fuck?"

Doing her best to remain calm and unnoticed by whatever crept in the shadows, she slowly reached and flipped the light switch on. She screamed. The corner was filled with crawling bugs. Being exposed, they started crawling in every direction. They were moving really fast and disappearing. Trista turned away to fumble through her vanity kit, looking for something she could use against them. She got ahold of a bottle of hairspray. When she turned back to face the threat, there was nothing. She made her way to the corner. Then she looked behind the toilet, the garbage, under the carpet, the towel rack... Nothing. She then spotted a tiny dark spot on the wall right in front of her. Somehow, she had missed the tiny single bug just being there. As if watching her or offering itself in sacrifice for the safety of its companions. Trista could hear the drum beat in her chest, announcing what seemed like a glimpse at a panic attack.

"I'm losing my fucking mind. Losing my mind over those FUCKING BUGS!" she screamed.

She screamed with all her will when she exterminated the bug under a layer of spray. Catching her breath, Trista sat on the toilet and then something broke inside her. She cried like she never had before. She dropped on the bathroom floor. Laying there, she cried, not even worrying about the bugs.

***

Five days passed. Trista was a wreck. Her apartment was a mess, her hygiene was worse. Her dad forced himself in to visit one day and she made her best to look alive just so he wouldn't worry too much and leave her alone. "Just a bad slope, I'll come around," she lied. She wouldn't even bother to eat, wash or watch her shows. She was always sleeping unless she went to the bathroom. Even the blade had started to show some rust, only adding to the prospect. The bugs came and went. Trista didn't care about them much either. Sitting on the toilet she wondered if and how long she could go like this before dying. The sad fact was that she couldn't wait. She hated life and she hated herself.

On her left, she noticed some crowded bugs jammed on the corner of the floor and the bathtub. They were motionless, like observing her next move. Then they slowly made their way towards the sink area and under the baseboard. Trista got up and followed them to the sink. Her eyes stopped at the blade. She picked it up. Her reflection was now hidden by the watermarks and the rust. She got on her knees and started cutting the edge of the baseboard. It gave in under pressure and she was able to rip a fair amount off the wall. The inside was covered in bugs, trying their best to hide as the light showed upon them. She could see their eggs too. After all, they were just like her in some ways. They just wanted to lay in darkness. But deep down she hated everything about it.

One last fight! she thought. She picked up the hairspray that was still lying on the floor. She then searched the medicine cabinet atop the sink and found a lighter. There was about an inch opening between the floor and wall. It was crawling with bugs. She flicked the lighter on and started to spray a flame at the bugs. She could almost hear them scream. A piece of insulation caught fire. Trista was in a trance. She cared nothing of the outcome.

Then something moved out of the accumulated dust. It looked like a tail or an antennae of some sort. It was organic, alive and it started screeching. Trista kicked herself up and fell backwards sitting on the toilet. For a brief moment, she was brought back from her reverie. Something was crawling inside the walls. Something big and angry. She could hear it move inside the walls all the way to the washer and dryer.

What she thought was an earthquake before, happened again. This time triple the intensity. Then everything became silent for a few seconds. Everything but the crackling fire slowly burning inside the wall. The power went out with a spark and the bathroom was suddenly only illuminated by the growing flames. Trista realized she was still holding the blade. She heard more commotion through the walls and then a loud bang.

The washing machine stumbled and then flew a few feet out of its slot. There was a big hole in the wall where it used to be. Slowly, two antennae emerged followed by a giant silverfish bug. It was surrounded by what must have been millions of its babies. *I am not seeing this... You're not real!* she thought. She was unable to move, speak or anything. The bug made its way to her. Standing in front of her, it arced its back upwards so that it was level with her.

The creature was as big as her. The antennae reached for her arms, then her legs. It was feeling her. It took hold of her, and Trista felt herself being dragged upwards. Like she was floating. She realized she wasn't afraid. As the bug approached with her pincer jaw wide open and bit her wrist, she lost all sensations. She dropped the blade in an already forming pool of blood. It was at that moment she felt something. She felt relieved. She closed her eyes, rested her head backwards and she smiled.

Unhinged

Jessica Gleason

Drip. Drip. Drip.

The rusted faucet of the Ext. 87 rest area never fully shuts off, droplets pooling in the partially clogged sink basin. Much like a moist clock ticking, the metered sound reverberates across the room, filling the silence and, hopefully, covering the sound of Randy's shallow breathing.

In. Out. In. Out. His breaths came quick, but he couldn't take a deep breath with his heart thumping so hard against his chest. Cool sweat beaded on his forehead and gathered in all of his dark crevasses as he tried to rationalize what he'd seen.

***

Randy sat, stretched uncomfortably in the inhospitable back seat of his Chevy Spark. The car saved him hundreds on gas, but it lacked the space to really stretch out and sleep. His trip back home was seventeen long hours through the boring pastoral Midwest, highways and cornfields, a less than riveting haul. When he started to nod off, swaying ever closer to the rail, Randy pulled off the road at the Ext. 87 rest area.

He enjoyed weekend visits with his boyfriend, but the commute was hell on his back. Half of the parking lot lights were operational, and he parked in one of the well-lit areas, great for safety, but not ideal for sleep.

Stepping out of the car, Randy stretched, fingertips extended as far as they'd go, shoulder cracking in the process. "There it goes," he said, before groaning and wandering towards the sparse facility. While there were a few other cars in the parking lot, the atrium was empty, quiet even, save the electronic buzzing of a handful of vending machines and a faint wet drop from further into the building.

"Fuck yeah, Mrs. Freshly's Oreo brownies!" Vending machines were usually a hard sell for Randy, his dairy allergy ruling out most of the common confections. He was over dry pretzels and hit the jackpot as the brownies were one of the few dairy free snack cakes out there.

As the spiral arm twisted, dropping the snack to the floor, Randy heard a thud and hushed squeal from deeper in the building. Curious, and lacking street smarts, he moved towards the sound instead of away from it.

Walk away man, walk away. This is how people get murdered. As he reached the back of the facility, there were only two directions in which to turn: left to the women's bathroom or right to the men's. Tilting his head ever so slightly, straining to hear, Randy could tell the dripping sound was definitely coming from the men's. No thuds, no squeals. Having to pee anyway, he wandered into the men's. Leaky faucet aside, it was a standard dingy restroom. Tiles were cracked and half the lights were operational, but he'd seen worse.

After relieving himself, Randy attempted to wash his hands, but finding no soap he had to settle for a lukewarm rinse and a thorough paper toweling. There's nothing weird here; go back to your car. Upon exiting the bathroom, Randy decided he'd wander towards the women's room just for good measure, curiosity driving his questionable decision making.

He padded his way across the breezeway, pausing to listen outside the other bathroom's opening. Nothing. Looking down, he noticed a thick smear of red sludge marring the gritty tile floor. *That can't be good. It's blood. I think it's blood.* Not wanting to alert any potential predators to his presence, he refrained from calling out, asking if someone needed help. But still he entered the room. Cautious and slow, hoping his tennis shoes wouldn't squeak on the floors as he went.

Heart thumping hard against his chest, rattling his ribcage, Randy peeked his head around the corner and into the bright room. Nothing. Three stalls, three sinks, and a few dispensers. The room was in slightly better condition than the one he'd just left, but it still wreaked of poor maintenance and eggy hard water. *Okay. It's empty. Leave. Go. Now.*

Instead of heeding his inner monologue, Randy felt compelled to do his due diligence. He crouched down, bending his head near to the ground, low enough to peek under the stalls. First stall, empty. Second stall, empty. Looking finally to the third stall, tucked in the corner of the room, Randy was relieved to not find anything out of place. *Whew.* Before standing, Randy heard a wet crunch emanating from somewhere in the room. Eyes still affixed to stall three, Randy bit his lip, stifling a scream when a severed hand was dropped to the floor, still leaking fluids. Before he managed to scramble up, a slender leg stepped down onto the floor. Whatever was in the stall wore black Mary Jane's and, for some reason, was in possession of a severed hand. Rushing backwards, jumping over the blood smeared near the entrance, Randy ran back to the men's room, diving into a stall and stepping carefully onto the toilet's rim. Mid-panic, he hadn't fully thought out his escape. Now trapped in the stall, he folded in on himself, full to the brim with panic and dread. *Shit.*

***

Dozens of thoughts raced through Randy's head. *Maybe she's hurt and it was her hand? That's stupid man, she'd be crying or something. No one loses a hand without crying, no one alive anyway. So, she's a murderer? She killed someone. Maybe she's done for the night. Maybe she'll leave. I just need to sit here and listen closely.* Drip.

Drip. Drip. *Until I hear footsteps and a door opening. That's all. Sit, calm down, run when she's gone.* Drip. Drip. Drip. *How am I supposed to hear anything with that stupid leaky faucet?* Drip. Drip. Drip.

Randy sat cross-legged on the less than sanitary toilet, willing his pulse to slow. After a few moments, his breaths came more regularly and he pulled his hands away from his mouth, trusting he could breathe quietly without needing to be muffled.

See, you're doing fine. Just a few more minutes and you can run to the Spark and get out of here. Drip. Drip. Drip. *What happened to the rest of the body? Something was dragged in there, right? Where did it go? Why was there only a hand?*

Amping himself up, fear rising, Randy's pulse quickened again, leaving him on the edge of panic, almost but not quite ready to tip over into an anxiety attack. Drip. Drip. Drip. He thought he heard a shuffle, but he couldn't be sure, not with the rhythmic water droplets pulling his focus every few seconds. Drip. Drip. Drip. *It's ok. You're fine. Calm down. It'll just be another minute or two.* Attempting to talk himself down, Randy froze when he heard the hard clack of fingernails tapping against concrete, likely the bathroom walls. *Shit. She's in here. Stay calm. Stay quiet.* Drip. Drip. Drip. Footsteps came closer and closer still, no longer attempting to be discreet. The woman was playing with him.

"I know you're in here," came a lilting feminine voice, ending her sentence with an upward inflection and a small giggle. "Don't you want to come out and play?"

Randy didn't move. He thought it might be a ploy; she didn't know, she wanted him to slip up and reveal himself. Drip. Drip. Drip.

So, holding his breath, he remained on the toilet, feeling as if his luck had run out. He could hear nails scratching their way across the stalls, moving closer to his hiding spot. "Excuse me, sir. I think it's time to come out now."

"No, go away." Voice shaking, he replied, giving up the hope that she'd just leave. Drip. Drip. Drip.

"I won't hurt you," the woman replied.

"I'm not about to trust that."

"You don't have much of a choice. This is the kind way, but if you won't come out, I'll rip the door from its hinges and I'll come in. We don't want that now, do we?"

Low on options, Randy was grateful he'd already emptied his bladder. He'd at least be spared the indignity of wetting himself in the face of this foe. *Why didn't I go back to my damn car?* He climbed down from his porcelain hiding spot, took a deep breath, unlatched the stall, and stepped out into the broken-down bathroom once again. Drip. Drip. Drip.

He hadn't had enough time to come up with an expectation, didn't know what he'd come face to face with once he crept into the main bathroom again. But the small, mousy, librarian of a woman wasn't what he expected. Drip. Drip. Drip. Her brown hair was neat, pulled up into a bun and she came complete with an off-white cardigan and a green pencil skirt. She raised one arm, waving, one finger at a time, in a slow-motion cascade. Her face, amused and smiling as Randy's face registered surprise.

"Excuse me, miss. I'm on my way out," he began, attempting to sidestep her and leave the room. But, she matched his footwork, blocking him each time. "Really, I have somewhere to be."

She looked up at him, still smiling. "Not anymore," she responded as her jaw cracked, unhinging, drooping down as her mouth became impossibly wide; rows upon rows of sharp teeth spiraled around her mouth and down into her throat.

"What the fuck?" Randy stood frozen; his feet unable to respond to the screaming in his brain. *Run. Now. Go.*

Her throat pouched out, a great gullet rounding out like a frog's buccal pouch, growing ever larger, basin-like, stretched lip forming a rim around her monstrous toilet-like cavity. Thick yellow mucus sloshed around in her toothy bowl as she moved nearer to Randy.

Attempting to talk, she said what sounded like, "spying is impolite," but he couldn't be sure as the sounds distorted when she attempted to spew words from her latrine mouth. Still immobile, Randy watched with sick fascination as she waddled closer with all of her sharp teeth. Drip. Drip. Drip.

Grabbing his hand and tugging, the woman threw off Randy's balance, shoving his arm into her waiting mouth. His skin was torn, snagging on hundreds of needle-like teeth before the burning began. Once his flesh hit the liquid, it began to bubble and crack, searing away the flesh and sending extreme pain signals to the center of Randy's brain. *This is it.* Drip. Drip. Drip. *The end.*

The woman chomped down, ripping his arm free, right at the shoulder. Randy stumbled back, gushing blood, smearing it into the floors as he scrambled to the wall. Looking over to his shoulder and the thick steady flow of blood, Randy disassociated.

The mousy, toilet-mouthed abomination moved closer to Randy's still form. Drip. Drip. Drip. This time going for the torso, craving vital organ meat, she tore into his stomach cavity, slurping out and devouring his intestines.

Randy's last thoughts weren't of his life's accomplishments or even of his loved ones; it wasn't his boyfriend's slender face that flashed across his dying brain. Instead, he had one thought, the brownie in his pocket. *I should have eaten that delicious bastard.* After a final bloody gasp, his heart gave out. The women made quick work of masticating his juicy flesh.

Once finished, her mouth began shrinking back down, deflating like a balloon with a slow leak. She belched, coughing up a few of Randy's fingers in the process. Once her bones had snapped back into place, she wiped any remaining blood from her lips and gave herself a once over in the mirror. "I look good," she said, before kicking Randy's fingers underneath the radiator unit and walking out the door, back to her Jetta, and then heading home to her two small children.

A Girl Alone at Night

Samantha Arthurs

As a general rule, Jessie made it a point to avoid stopping anywhere late at night if she was traveling alone. The world was an unsafe place, even more so if you were a woman on your own, and she was not a person who took a lot of risks in life. Which was why she'd been fighting so hard to calm down her stomach as she traveled the winding, and vastly empty, old state highway she had to take back to the interstate when leaving Lucy's house. They'd had another game night, and this time there had been Mexican food. She had known when she'd eaten that it could be a potentially bad idea, and she felt it more with every mile.

There were few places on the road to stop, especially at this time of night, but there was one lone gas station about fifteen miles from the exit she'd take to get back to real civilization. There was just no way she could make it that fifteen miles, let alone another ten from their home. So, she was forced to pull over at an old Shell station, pulling up alongside one of the ancient looking pumps.

It was an old place, the sort that probably should have given up the ghost and closed long before now. There were four pumps, though two of them were covered up to insinuate they were no longer operational. There was no cover over the island either, just a few tall streetlights to illuminate the area. The pavement was chipping up in places and deeply oil stained in others, and the smell of it all left something to be desired. The station was also woefully small, with a sign promising a bathroom around the corner. It was there that she had been greeted by a second sign, telling her to see the attendant for the key.

Jessie had finally procured the key, which was attached to an actual wooden ruler to apparently prevent theft or loss, from the bored-looking teenaged boy behind the register. He hadn't even looked up from whatever he was watching on his tablet, feeling around beneath the counter for the key and just sliding it over to her. She couldn't remember if she'd even mumbled a "thank you" as she'd made her way back outside to the side of the building where the restroom was.

She was in there now, pants around her ankles and arms wrapped around her ailing stomach as it began to rid itself of what had angered it. She was willing herself to just stare at her shoes, and not look around. It was impossible to just keep her eyes on her Keds though, and she caught herself taking in the surroundings.

Gas stations bathrooms were, for the most part, usually somewhat disgusting. This one, however? This one took the cake for possibly the worst she had ever seen. The single bare bulb overhead illuminated the grimy, mint green walls in such a way that she could see every smudge and smear. There were plenty, that was for certain, and some of them more questionable than others. There were the standard names and phone numbers scrawled here and there, and places where people had scraped the paint completely off the walls.

The tile floor was dingy and cracking in places, and the grout hadn't been cleaned in, oh, fifty years or so. Wet toilet paper had dried in the corners and around the drain, which told Jessie that this bathroom had flooded, more than once, and likely hadn't been sanitized after the fact. The sink, however, was the worst offender. The nooks and crannies around the drain, faucet, and knobs were black with years of untouched filth, speckled with little flecks of rust besides. The faucet dripped steadily, plink, plink, plink, having worn off the original white enamel coating where the drips landed to reveal a brassy color underneath.

Nobody had taken out the trash, there was no soap, and very little of what looked to be single ply toilet paper. A slight breeze came from around the door, let in by a good half inch gap around the lock where someone had tried to pry it open at some point. She could see outside through the crack, though there wasn't anything to see besides the orange light of the outside night light that hung above the door.

Jessie told herself to just take some deep breaths (as deep as she dared considering), and get through it. This was an emergency, and she could take a hot shower when she got home to wipe off the feeling of this place. Next time she ventured out to Lucy's, she'd be sure to watch what she ate, so this same unfortunate mistake didn't happen again. It was bad enough to have to stop somewhere like this in the middle of the night anyway, let alone having to take a risk like that twice.

She was still in the midst of her body expelling her tacos, though the cramping had eased up considerably, when someone banged loudly on the door. Jessie had zoned out finally, watching a centipede crawling across the floor near one of the toilet paper mounds in the corner, so the loud noise startled her. She jumped, her in her throat, taking a moment to get her bearings.

"Someone's in here! Didn't the kid inside tell you?" Jessie called out, noting that the orange light from outside was now being blocked by the person standing on the other side of the door. "I'll be just a few more minutes!"

No answer came, but the person shuffled away. Jessie heard their feet on the concrete sidewalk, and the light returned from outside via the door gap. She started to rub her face with her hands, thought the better of it, and instead began to unwind the thin toilet paper while silently praying it would be enough. Rubbing her stomach, she concluded she was pretty much done and got to her feet, ready to wrap this ordeal up and get home.

Jessie heard running feet first, and then somebody practically slamming into the door. She let out an involuntary scream this time, almost tripping over her pants which were still around her ankles. She managed not to make a mess of herself in the process of finishing up, reaching down to hitch up her pants as the person began to bang again, but this time more persistently.

"I'm almost done," she practically shouted, turning on the hot water tap. Nothing came out so switched to cold, trying to quickly wash her hands. The banging just continued, starting to feel grating to the point that she reached over with her own fist and whacked the door in return. "Cut it OUT! I hear you!"

There was a pause from the other side, and then the banging turned to tapping. It sounded like the person was now drumming their fingers on the door, and that made a strange tingle travel down Jessie's spine. It was almost midnight, in the middle of nowhere. Yes, this was the only gas station she knew of before the interstate rest areas, but something about the situation started to feel wrong. Maybe it felt wrong because it was a creepy gas station in the middle of nowhere, and she was a woman by herself. Or, perhaps, she had watched one too many slasher films. Whatever the reason, Jessie knew right then that she wasn't opening the door until the person on the other side of it got lost.

"Hey," she called out then, moving to stand right in front of the door. "You're giving me the creeps, okay? I'm not coming out until you go, so you may as well just find another place to pee!"

The drumming continued, and Jessie got the picture pretty quickly that this wasn't going to go how she had hoped. Lowering the toilet seat she sat down on top of it, staring at the gap in the door again. She couldn't see anything, the light effectively blocked out, and she wondered how long the person out there could keep up the charade. She was frightened, that was pretty obvious, and if that was their objective then what more did they want from her?

Jessie wasn't sure she wanted an answer to the question, stomach turning now for a reason completely unrelated to dinner. A faint orange glow caught her eye then, and she almost sighed with relief. The light was back! That meant they were leaving, didn't it? They would go, she'd wait a few beats, and then bolt for her car. To hell with the key or that pimply faced teenager inside waiting to have it back. She was done with this place, and she was getting out of her.

It took a moment for the shock to register as the light moved again, though it wasn't replaced by the darkness of someone standing in front of the gap. No, there was an eye looking back at her, and it was like her brain couldn't compute at first. When it did, the scream that erupted from her was shrill, and shocked even herself. She had never screamed like that in her life, a scream of true fright, instinctively lifting her legs up off the floor to pull her knees close to her chest.

The person on the other side of the door, the person now looking at her, laughed then. It wasn't a pleasant laugh ever, nothing jovial at all in its tone. No, this was sinister and unhinged, the kind of laugh that made Jamie's heart start to pound. She didn't look away though, keeping her gaze on the door and the person who was watching her, clearly amused by the fear they were instilling.

"Little pig, little pig," the person whispered, just loud enough to be audible through the gap. Jessie couldn't tell whether it was more or female, the volume and pitch too faint for her to tell. "Let me in."

"Go away," Jessie stammered out, sucking in a deep breath of air to keep herself from being sick from the fear. "Just go, please! I just want to go home!"

"Doesn't everyone?" The person asked then, followed by another one of those strange, manic laughs. Carefully, almost reverently, they leaned back then and slid two of their fingers into the gap, wiggling them a little. They couldn't quite reach though, couldn't quite make it past the edge of the door frame.

When they tried the knob Jessie just moaned in despair, sliding off the toilet seat and onto the filthy floor. She tucked herself into the corner between the sink and toilet, trying to make herself small. As though being smaller might somehow save her from this moment, from that person out there. The fingers were pulled back, disappearing from the gap so the light returned. Seconds ticked by, then minutes, and there was silence now. Jessie was too scared to move, flinching involuntarily when a small roach crawled over the toe of her shoe, disappearing into a crack in the wall. Slowly she began to feel hope that it was over, but then there came a scraping sound. Metal on metal. Unsettling and upsetting, once Jessie realized what was going on.

Something was being wedged into the gap, between the door and the frame. They were moving it around and tapping at the bolt with it, trying to get the door open. Had they done this before? Were they the person who had dented the door to begin with? Jessie didn't know, but the thought of them getting inside made her tremble. There was nothing in here to use as a weapon, not so much as a plunger, and she had foolishly left her phone in the car in her hurry to get inside.

The car. She remembered her keys then, tugging them from her pocket. Her last hope was this, smashing her thumb against the alarm button as hard as she could.

Nothing happened.

She was too far away from the car, which was parked at the front of the station at the gas pumps. It was also possible that all the concrete block of the building kept the signal from permeating, leaving her stranded here with nothing. Her brain began to churn, trying to think quickly as the person kept working at the door. The cashier! There was someone on the other side of this wall technically, and while he was a distracted teenager, he would hear her!

Jessie began to scream then, as loud as she could and for all she was worth. Her adrenaline spiked, hoping beyond anything she'd ever hoped before that the kid would hear her. "Help! HELP ME! I'm in the bathroom, someone is after me! HELP!"

There was nothing. Just more horrifying silence, broken only by the scraping of metal on metal. Jessie curled up again, burying her head in her knees. She counted to herself slowly, trying to stay calm. How long had it been? She didn't know, she didn't have a watch. Now and then she smelled cigarette smoke, the person on the other side taking breaks from their work to indulge. Once or twice they walked away, but both times they came back. They'd watch her through the gap, or try to wedge their fingers in again. Once or twice they sang her soft, nonsense songs that made her skin crawl.

When they'd stop their tinkering with trying to pry the gap wider or fidget with the lock, they'd go back to knocking. The sound felt like it was echoing inside of Jessie's skull, making her skin crawl. She tried putting her hands over her ears, but that didn't shut out the noise. It got even worse when she finally got the sense about her to turn off the bare bulb overhead, preventing them from looking at her.

"Little pig," the person whispered, right up against the gap now. "No, no, no. Naughty."

"Why me? Why do this to me?" Jessie asked then, voice cracking. She wanted to cry now, as it became increasingly evident that this nightmare was never going to end. "What's wrong with you!"

"Wrong with me?" they asked from the other side, back to drumming their fingers again. "Nothing is wrong with me. Why you? Because...why not? You were here. That's reason enough."

She broke then, a few sobs escaping her. They seemed to enjoy that, renewed in their efforts to pry open the door, working hard and more feverishly. Jessie cried until her head began to throw, reaching up to turn the knob on the sink. She splashed cold water on her face and then curled back up again, shivering a little. The night was getting colder, and that coldness was creeping in now. She felt it through the thin canvas of her shoes, and the light material of her yoga pants.

Jessie went back to counting, as the night dragged on. At some point the adrenaline had faded, the fear had melted away, and she'd fallen asleep there, wedged between a dirty sink and an old, leaking toilet that ran nearly continuously. Once or twice, she jerked away as the person pulled hard on the door or slammed against it, but the lock held. The place might have been dirty, but nobody could say it wasn't well built.

When Jessie woke up, it was to the door being thrown wide open and early morning light spilling into the bathroom. She was still curled up in the corner, head resting against the toilet tank. A short, balding man in a tank top and a tall, stern-faced police officer were both staring at her in confusion.

"Young lady. How long have you been in here?" The cop asked her, watching as Jessie crawled out of her safe space and pulled herself to her feet. "What in the hell went on here last night? We got a dead cashier inside the store, a stolen car in the parking lot, and now we got you hiding out in the shitter."

"Did you see who killed Davey?" That question came from the balding man, who looked both shocked and concerned. "I'm the owner. I came in this morning to take over, found him dead right there at the register! Ma'am?"

Jessie hadn't said anything, just stared as the two men asked her if she knew what had happened here. Finally, she pushed past them, and took in several deep breaths of fresh, morning air. The sidewalk outside the bathroom was littered with cigarette butts, a couple of empty beer bottles, and a heavy looking hunting knife with the tip broken off the blade. Had that been what they'd tried to use on the door? She didn't know, and she'd tell the officer and the small balding man just that. First though, she had to make one thing perfectly clear.

"I'll tell you everything I know. I promise. I just had to get out of that fucking bathroom."

The Demon of Monroe Street

Steven Haupt

I'm writing this, as it may be the final thing I do. Strange things have been happening to me of late and I fear my time may be growing near. I must share how this all happened.

It was a few months ago. You see, I accepted a strange job, one that many would find to be too much for them to handle. I am what most people would call a ghost hunter, though I consider paranormal investigator to be the more professional term. I work with a priest, Bruce. He and I have been friends for decades, ever since we were children.

Before I joined him, I was someone who was quite experienced with cinematography, photographic cameras, video cameras, lights, microphones, things of that nature. I worked under the director on a television show for a number of years. So, he asked me to bring some of my equipment and help him capture his investigations. I agreed, not fully believing in ghosts. I figured it would mostly be something of a television show, dramatized. You see, I worked on a horror movie before, a film about demons taking over people. It was difficult to actually believe it after I saw behind the scenes and was a part of creating the illusion for the camera.

We are called upon when there is a disturbance at a home or school, residential or commercial places like that usually. We find what is causing the paranormal activity, identify it, retrieve evidence, and sometimes if we can, get rid of it. When I explain my career choice to most people, I always get the same first response. They always ask about the evidence. Mostly, if I have any footage or pictures to show them.

Assuming whomever is reading this is asking the same question, let me explain a little more in depth by telling the story of my first case ever as a paranormal investigator. It was a family in a new home. They told us that within a week of them moving into their new home, they began experiencing things: kitchen cupboards slamming, lights turning on and off, sometimes the children said they would see a shadow figure standing at the foot of their beds or in their closets.

Bruce and I went over to the home when the family was away. This made it easier to conduct our investigation. Being new to the job, I just followed him around and carried a load of equipment as we walked through the house. I brought whatever I could if I thought it would help capture the events that were occurring.

Bruce didn't walk around with a cross, or with a rosary, anything like that. He walked only carrying a flashlight and a journal. This journal had a list of different types of paranormal beings, what they tend to do, what they like, dislike, and things like that to help him determine what it was we were dealing with. At this point though, I was still quite skeptical of it all.

I carried something called an EMF reader as we walked; Bruce gave it to me. It's a small device that beeps and lights up when it detects electromagnetic fields in the area. As explained to me by Bruce, this was only one of the many ways to not only find where the specter resides in the home, but it also helps identify it. He claims that some types of specters cannot be detected while others can.

After we entered a room, we would turn on a light, so that we knew we had been there. Bruce would pull out a standard infrared thermometer as well, to check the temperature of each room we entered. Some specters prefer the freezing cold and lower the temperature drastically in whatever room they reside in.

We had checked the entire house and found no changes in temperature, no EMF reading, and no activity of any kind. Because of this lack of evidence, it was impossible to determine where and what the specter was.

There was one door still shut, the one place we hadn't gone to, and if I'm being honest, it was the one place I dreaded the most as I feel most people would, especially for their first time. The place I spoke of, was of course the basement. We swung open the door, and it squealed and creaked as if it hadn't been open for years. Bruce called out to me. "Spirit box," he said. That's a radio device that scans through the frequencies and will allow the spectator to speak directly to you, something I found to be quite drastic.

It emitted a horrible static sound as it went through the FM radio frequencies. We crept down the stairs and into the dark basement. There was a long hallway and at the end of it was an open door to a bathroom. Bruce pulled on a long string that turned the swinging light on. It was the only light in the hallway.

As I pointed the EMF reader at the bathroom and got closer, it began to beep. My heart skipped a beat as it went from one to three, then to five. I could feel the temperature drastically decline as I neared the bathroom. Suddenly, I heard a loud beeping sound. I looked down at the light of the EMF reader flickering. It went from one to five, up and down. That's when the specter revealed itself to us.

A black shadow crawled on its hands and feet out of the bathtub onto the floor. I saw its horns, its long tongue, and hooved feet. It burst with speed towards us but stopped just before it hit us. It began laughing, all around us, laughing.

Bruce quickly turned the light back on and asked if I was alright. He demanded that I hand him the bag of things I had brought in. He withdrew two crucifixes and placed one near us, and the other near the bathroom door. He then pulled out his journal and began writing in it. I later learned he was writing down the evidence we had gotten to help determine what the specter was. He got the spirit box again and began talking into it, asking it questions.

The light of the bathroom flickered on and off and the tub began to fill. It wasn't water pouring from the spout though, it was what I could only determine to be blood. I pulled out the photographic camera we brought and began taking photos of the bathroom. I could hear Bruce ask it its name, to which it replied that it was going to kill us. It began speaking what I think was Latin, but I'm not quite sure.

Bruce demanded that it leave this place, and if it wouldn't willingly then he would make it. Again, it laughed loudly. The tub overflowed and the mirror above the sink cracked. The lights all burst, and the spirit box turned off.

I tried my flashlight, but it wouldn't work. So, thinking quickly on my feet, I took a photo. The flash was quite bright and showed the entirety of the bathroom. I took another... and another. The crucifix lit ablaze, and Bruce began calling out to the spectator once again, demanding it to leave.

I took another photo; I really don't know why. I suppose it was so that we could see, but at the same time, all I remember was not wanting to see anything. I wanted to close my eyes, but of course, I didn't.

I took the photo and whatever it was stood in the doorway, filling it with its shadowy frame. It seemed angry, as if it was sick of playing with us and now wanted us to go home. Without it even leaving its domain, the bathroom, it forced me closer to it. I had no control of myself. I was dragged in as if a rope was attached to my ankles and it was pulling me.

It lifted me up and held onto me. Bruce tried to enter the bathroom, but the door slammed shut and locked him out. The tiny bathroom slowly began to grow larger. Far larger than any bathroom I had ever seen. It was playing tricks on my mind. It dragged me across the extended bathroom to the cracked mirror. The mirror took up nearly the whole wall above the counter where the sink was.

The specter threw me down on the hard tile. It climbed up onto the counter and dug its fingers into the crack of the mirror. It began ripping and tearing away the glass. I'll never forget what I saw, the horror of it. It was hell, a fiery chasm of death and despair.

It grabbed my arm and then entered the shredded mirror. It began pulling me in until Bruce swung open the bathroom door and began yelling at it to unhand me. He threw a vile of holy water at it, held a crucifix up with one hand and a bible and rosary in the other. He began reading, but I couldn't hear a word he was saying. It was all just noise to me. I fought with all of my strength to get free from its grasp.

A strange feeling crept over me as I stared into the black abyss of its eyes. I felt lighter, weaker, and to this day I can only describe it as my soul being ripped from me. I began slipping from its grasp and the portal I suppose you could call it, began to seal back up. Bruce pressed the crucifix against its wrist. I yanked away, but as I did, it left three claw marks in my flesh. The mark of this beast.

I looked inside the small opening one last time to see the pits of hell and the specter that took me. It was trying to force itself back in, trying to take me again. I threw myself backwards into the wall of the now small bathroom. As the mirror sealed shut, it severed a finger from the specter. I picked it up and put it in my pocket.

Bruce lit a strange bundle of sticks of some kind that produced an odd smelling smoke and waved it around the bathroom. He splashed holy water all over, blessing it. Finally, he placed a cross on the countertop beside the sink and we left.

When we got to the car, Bruce explained to me what it was. He was pale in the face. When he told me I recall my stomach turning. I felt sick. He told me it was a demon. I asked him, pleaded with him to make sure it was gone from the house. He assured me the house was safe again.

Later that night I noticed a strange marking on my wrist where the claw marks were. A small symbol I couldn't recognize. I never told Bruce about the mark, but maybe I should have. Bruce passed away last week. At his wake I felt the same sick feeling in my stomach that I felt all those years ago. I saw the same mark in the same place on his wrist, that I had on mine.

The thought of this demon following us... maybe it's what killed Bruce. It prompted me to write this. I fear I'm next and I have been avoiding my impending doom for too long. With Bruce now gone it's only a matter of time. I can no longer bear the waiting. As I sleep in bed, I see its figure in the bathroom, staring at me as I sleep. When I gaze into my mirror for too long, I begin to see hell again, as if I was looking at it through a window.

I have tried all I can to rid myself of this demon. I have blessed myself and home. I've moved several times, but I can no longer. Every bathroom I enter has a mirror and, in that mirror, I gaze into the pits of hell, watching that demon look back at me, laughing, waiting for me.

We only did a few more cases after that, before Bruce's sudden death. No other case matched that of the demon on Monroe Street. It has been with both of us this whole time; it marked us. I fear neither of us were prepared for what we came across that day. Goodbye... I know not what is on the other side for me, I only hope it isn't what I saw in the bathroom mirror.

Focus

Melinda Finholm Morris

I'd been reclining in this arctic tub for... honestly, I don't know how long. I take long and luxurious baths often, but this was different. It felt different. For one, my submerged body was beyond freezing; I was numb from my shoulders to my toes. My neck registered the tundra-like temperature and the frigidity seemed to have slowed my brain. I hate the cold. Secondly, I don't remember drawing a bath. This was not my tub. My thoughts were still hazy, like I was trying to wake up. Poking through the fog were incessant and erratic questions. Where was I? What house? What time was it? Who made the ridiculous color choice for these bathroom walls? What day was it? Why did it hurt to stretch? What was that smell? Where is Iza?

Stop squirreling and dig in. Focus. What do I know to be true? I am Jen. I am a senior at Valdosta State University. I am 22. My. Head. Hurts. I have a masseuse job lined up. I am afraid. I am cold. I am confused. I don't know where I am, what I'm doing here, or how I got here. I like furry animals. I do not black out and wake up in bathtubs. Clubs don't have bathtubs. Dammit, I can't hear my thoughts over the pounding of my heart. What is that smell?

Focus. What can I control? Myself. Breathe. Deep breath belly rise... breathe out belly fall. Fill my lungs, what was it... box breaths. Yeah, I need to think. I need to calm the fuck down. I can't think when I'm panicking. Calm is a superpower. I can figure this out. Okay, I'm ready to think. Focus. What was the last thing I could remember? My head was pounding as I searched my distorted memory bank. I closed my eyes to shut out the dying soft white lights from the vanity and concentrated.

I knew I made plans to go clubbing with my friend Iza; she was the life of the party and brought me out of my shell. I donated my precious O positive blood that morning. It was always drilled into me that I'm in high demand and blood is life. Besides, I could get drunk faster the day I gave blood. It's a bonus - save the world, cheaper buzz. Iza and I agreed we needed to unwind from the constant, increasing requirements jammed into our packed schedules before graduation. Our biology degrees were almost a milestone of the past. Our adulting badges were waiting, and we were ready.

Iza. She saved me. I was so lost my freshman year. Being in the same program and same dorm gave her many opportunities to slowly erode my inhibitions and cautious nature. Now, we go out to the same club almost every Friday night.

Focus. Remember. As usual, I arrived at our normal rendezvous spot before Iza and decided to get my own party started. I was sure she would catch up with me - she always did. I acknowledged some other regulars on my way to the bar to order my Long Island Iced Tea. It was that kind of night; no martini derivative or fruity cocktail would do. *Oy vey, why did I use alcohol to unwind?* My mom's irritating voice barged into my recollection process to remind me about the importance of healthier coping mechanisms and personal holistic resilience. I heard that message for so long, a by-product of being a therapist's kid. Maybe I did it to throw up the middle finger at her. Maybe it was my desire to let alcohol suppress my frontal lobe - *take that, Mom!* I know what alcohol does and I choose those effects. I had enough with rational thinking. I needed a break. Our usual bartender wasn't there to catch up, but I didn't care. I am not a fan of small talk anyway.

Wait, what was that noise? I jarringly came back to the present and heard what sounded like panicked shuffling and cabinets banging somewhere close to my proximity. There were no voices to clue me in to who was around. Who were they? Friends or foes? Is there one person or more? And why was the water so cold? I hate the cold. Why was I in the tub? Should I call out for help? What was that smell?

Focus. I've heard ice baths are good for training recovery, but I also read they were not supposed to exceed fifteen minutes. And, I hadn't done a traditional workout in over a year. *What the hell?* I didn't see ice, but I damn sure know it is not relaxing. I am not relaxed. I'm alarmed. I'm terrified. I'm alone. *Where is Iza? Is she okay?* I'm too tired to think, I'll just rest my eyes for a quick second.

Wait, I know that voice! It's Kyle, he works at the blood lab I donate to every sixteen weeks. He is so efficient, handsome, and capable - I never feel the prick of the needle when I donate with him. He always seems happy to see me and makes sure I get Oreos on the way out, especially if there aren't any on the counter.

"Kyle!" I tried to scream, but it came out as a raspy whisper. How had I not noticed my throat hurt? Why was it hard to swallow? I didn't have strep throat or a cold, what was causing the discomfort? I realized that nothing bound my body or my hands or feet. I moved in the water raising my arms up the sides slowly and noticed brown surgical bandages on my torso. My stomach had an orange hue. As the water sloshed, I heard Kyle curse and yell at someone else in another room about the 'damn sedative dosage'.

Wait, what? Sedative? I have never had surgery or been hospitalized, ever. *What the fuck do I need a sedative for? Why is Kyle here? Who is he with?* We never hung out, despite my endless high context romantic overtures that were maybe not obvious to him, flirtatious hints I wouldn't mind exploring our options. He never picked up what I was putting down.

Over the years and pints of blood, I'd told Kyle about my grades, goals, frustrations with my mom, invited him to come out with me and Iza, and my hobbies and interests. He seemed to be interested in me beyond the health questionnaire. He asked if I traveled to other countries, if I had any siblings, why I do not talk about my extended family much, if I'd had any surgeries, and if I was a loner. I shared it had really just been me and Mom growing up and she worked a lot. I like to be alone most of the time, but I found space for Iza in my bubble. Iza pushed me out of my solitude, and we always went to the same club to unwind. Iza was my closest friend.

Focus. I collected myself, placed my hands on the smooth edges and started to push myself to rise from the tub. Peering over the side I noticed Iza on the floor. Her brunette hair was matted and messy. She was on her back, arms to the side, palms were up, fingers slightly curled in. Her mouth was slightly parted, and except for the surgical bandages taped randomly over her dark orange hued abdomen, she was completely naked. Her soulless eyes looked in my direction like she was trying to tell me something. I realized I'd never hear her voice again. Her message was incomplete. I was incomplete.

I froze. I couldn't take my eyes away from her empty hazel eyes. *Foe! These are foes! Not friends. Not helpful. Not safe. NOT SAFE.* I reminded myself to breathe. Use my senses. Focus. Look around. My mind was racing. Was there anything I could use as a weapon? No. Were my clothes in here? No. Were my legs working? Could I move? Yes.

Wait. Kyle. He was still yelling at the unknown companion. I had time. I tried not to slosh the water as I lifted out of the tub. My balance was slightly off; I couldn't trust my feet because I could barely feel them. I put one foot on the floor. *Damn!* No rug, no carpet and it was slick. I grabbed the shower curtain - thank God it held. *Steady, steady. Quiet. Other foot.* The bath looks harmless. Like any other one after a bath - no blood, no hints to treachery, pain, or death.

Bleach! That is what I smelled. Identifying the smell gave me a boost of confidence and control.

Focus. Look around. Iza, Iza! I don't know what happened, I'm so sorry! Gingerly stepping around my friend's physical shell, I sat on the toilet. The toilet plunger could be useful for something. *At least it's something.* I wrapped my right hand around the plunger and picked it up. Working up the courage, avoiding eye contact with Iza, I lifted myself off the toilet and worked my way toward the door.

Holding the plunger in my right hand, I started to turn the doorknob with my left. I could not care that I was naked or that my abdomen was sore. Based on the placement of the bandage, thanks to my human biology class, I knew it was near my kidney. My kidney. My O positive, likely to match other people's transplant needs kidney. *Oh. My. God! We were being harvested!* I am all about consent and I DID NOT GIVE IT.

Focus. I was starting to get feeling back in my body and I was not a fan of the pins and needles feeling, even though I was a fan of being alive. Alive. Would I be alive much longer? Yes.

I took a deep breath and opened the door to see Kyle's surprised face looking back at me. As a cloth went over my face, my senses failed me. I don't remember ever leaving that bathroom.

It Came From the Pipes

Radar DeBoard

Amy pushed her way through the clustered group of people blocking the hallway entrance. They paused only momentarily as she pushed some of them out of her way, before continuing their conversation. It was late enough into the party and she had no doubt they were already trashed, so her minor indiscretion would probably be forgotten in a few minutes. Regardless, her mind was solely focused on reaching the bathroom and not on making sure she was being polite. The moment she pushed passed the final person, she was met by the near darkness of the hallway, thanks to most of the lights in the apartment being switched off to set the mood for the party. So, she was left to stumble down the dark corridor while feeling along the right wall for a door.

Once her fingers touched wood, she wasted no time in locating the knob and throwing the door open. She immediately fumbled about for the light switch of the bathroom, being sure to flip it on before slamming the door behind her. A tightness gripped her chest as sweat rolled down the side of her cheeks. Frantically, she turned on the sink, taking the water that came from the faucet and flinging it onto her face. Amy didn't even notice she was breathing heavily until she spied her reflection in the mirror and caught sight of her chest rapidly moving. This only reaffirmed what she already knew, she was having a panic attack. Her anxiety had gotten the better of her at the worst possible time, and she needed to calm down.

As she turned and locked the door, making sure no one could find her in such a distressing state, she silently berated herself. Why hadn't she taken her anxiety meds before heading to the party? Just because she wouldn't be able to drink? It was a stupid reason, and now it probably ruined the night for her. To make things worse, she had driven there, and with five mixed drinks in the past two hours, there was no way she could drive in her current state. The reality of the situation was that she had to come down from the panic attack and somehow become sober enough to drive, all in the span of a few minutes before someone banged on the door to use the bathroom.

She gripped the edge of the sink with all her might as the situation overwhelmed her mind. Desperately, she tried to regain control of her thoughts but found the struggle was almost too much to handle. Amy glanced up at herself in the mirror, making eye contact with her reflection. That helped to ground her in the moment and gave her just enough control of the situation to take the initial step toward calming down. The first thing she focused on was her breathing, deliberately stopping the quick, erratic ones she had been taking in, and transitioned to slow, long ones instead. After only a few seconds of this, she started to feel slightly better and her iron-tight grip on the sink loosened a bit.

As her heart rate gradually slowed and she finally calmed, Amy tried to remember what had brought on the panic attack. She recollected standing in the kitchen simply talking with a few friends and then...then she was frantically trying to make it to the bathroom. There was clearly something missing from her memory, and it annoyed the hell out of her. She placed all her attention on trying to recall the missing piece of information that had caused her to freak out, turning over every detail of the last fifteen or so minutes. Though, the more effort she put toward it, the harder it seemed to come up with anything. As she was about to give up, something clicked and the hidden moment came back to her.

The thing that had caused her to flip out was that familiar feeling, the one that had plagued her for the past year. That strange sensation of something sinister creeping up on her, wanting to do her harm... it had caught Amy off guard in the kitchen. It felt like something was mere inches away from attacking her, but like all the times she had experienced the terror-inducing sensation, she knew that wasn't true. There was never anything there, and there never would be. It was just a feeling and nothing more. She had told herself hundreds of times that nothing evil was coming for her, and yet, that feeling persisted. Despite how many times she proved to herself that nothing was there, that terrible feeling kept coming back.

Regardless, with her understanding of what had happened, she could finish calming down. Once Amy felt relaxed enough to pivot her focus, she turned her attention to the issue of her intoxication. As she tried to come up with some quick way to sober up, a sudden rumbling from the toilet caught her attention. Curiosity naturally took hold of her, and she leaned toward the toilet to see what had caused the sound. Several moments of stillness passed and just as she thought there was nothing to worry about, something shot up out of the porcelain bowl, splashing water everywhere.

Amy stumbled back into the door while a strange substance fell to the floor. She wiped the water off her face before looking down at the tile to find a strange, pink goo lying there. Her gaze followed the puddle of gunk laying on the floor, finding it connected to a strand of the nasty-looking substance that led into the toilet. Utterly confused by what she was staring at, Amy simply stood there while trying to comprehend what lay before her. Suddenly, a part of the goo shot forth from the puddle and landed on her shoe. In a knee-jerk reaction, she tried shaking the substance off, but it clung to her footwear. Mere moments later, more of the slime leapt forward, attacking her shoe while remaining attached to the initial puddle on the floor.

Fear overwhelmed Amy and she frantically kicked even harder at the pink gunk to no avail. Desperation took over and without thinking clearly, she decided to attack the puddle itself. She brought down her foot that was not already covered in goo, onto the pile of the strange substance, only to be met with a wet thud. When her attack didn't work, she tried to pull her foot free of the puddle but found it was stuck. In an instant, the pink substance rocketed up her caught foot and enveloped her leg up to the knee. Gripped with fear, she cried out for help, but the loud music of the party filling the rest of the apartment seemed to drown out her shouts.

A sudden but forceful tug came from the bit of goo that had grabbed her leg and Amy fell to the floor. At the end of the plummet, she hit her head on the floor, which stunned her while the gunk tugged on her leg once more. As she lay there, her head throbbing in pain, she noticed a stinging sensation coming from her enveloped appendage. Amy glanced at her leg and found the part of her pants that were surrounded by the slime were being eaten away. A sinking feeling hit her gut as she realized the gunk was eating away at her clothes, and soon, her body. There came a third tug from the sentient substance, and this time it was strong enough to pull Amy a few inches across the floor. It took only a second for it to become clear to her that the goo was trying to drag her to the toilet.

She struggled to fight against the pull, frantically grabbing at everything around her, but the smooth surface of the tile offered nothing to grip. The substance continued to eat away at her clothing and had begun to work on dissolving her skin. Agony shot through Amy's leg while the gunk worked itself up her body enveloping more of her. The tugging became stronger with each passing moment, and soon she felt her foot brush against the porcelain bowl. In between the unbearable agony and flailing for survival, she asked herself what this thing was and where it had come from.

As the gunk forcefully pulled her leg into the bowl, the answers dawned on her. That horrible feeling, she couldn't seem to get rid of for the past year? It was a warning, trying to tell her about this pink slime. This creature had been stalking her, hiding in the pipes, waiting for its chance to take her. That's why she never found what the sensation had been warning her about, because it hid in the plumbing, following her wherever she went. These terrible realizations only added to the unbearable dread tearing away at Amy while the sludge yanked her leg, slamming it against the hole in the bottom of the bowl.

The pain in her leg as the top of her skin started to dissolve was excruciating, but it was about to get far worse. With inhuman-like strength, the gunk pulled her foot against the hole with such force that it crushed the appendage, breaking all the bones in her foot to the point where it slid into the pipe. Amy wailed in agony, her mind going blank from the pain while the pink goo forcefully pulled more of her leg down the hole of the toilet. Further tugging brought her knee to the mouth of the hole, but of course, it was too large to fit down it. This didn't stop the gunk from pulling with enough power that the bone in the knee itself broke, sending shockwaves of agony throughout Amy's body.

As her knee was forcefully pulled into the hole, the pain became too much to handle, and Amy blacked out. Her body went limp, which did nothing but make it easier for the pink goo to pull more of her into the toilet. Thankfully, she wasn't awake for when her pelvis was smashed and broken to fit through the small opening. The creature didn't stop until all of Amy had been crushed down and pulled into the piping leading off from the toilet. In total, the horrific process took only ten minutes, and nothing was left behind but several puddles of water. Meaning, none would be the wiser, and no one would ever know what had happened to Amy.

The Seventh Death

Kim Fielding

The sixth time that Raymond died was disappointing.

A foot stepping too quickly on a wet tile floor, a windmilling loss of balance, a heavy fall, a head cracking against the edge of the cast iron bathtub, a neck broken. Within seconds there was nothing but a sprawled, cooling body, its eyes wide in blind startlement.

There should have been jets of blood or agonized chest-clutching. Terrified begging devolving to wordless screams. Even the desperate grasp at life as lungs failed under water or the brain faded under pharmaceuticals, those final moments of hope reaching up and then dissolving.

But this time there was only Raymond in the dissipating steam of the bathroom, watching.

Eventually there would be a shocked discovery, perhaps with some gasping and trembling. That would be nice. But it would be quickly followed by tedious removal and cleaning, and then everything would be quiet and dull again.

But that was all right. Raymond knew how to wait. And with any luck, his next death would be more interesting.

***

Alden Webb stood in the parlor of the inn, waiting impatiently to be checked in. Music wafted in from somewhere, a Doors song that had been popular a few years ago: The End. The irony didn't escape him.

"What brings you to our town, Mr. Webb?"

He smiled tightly at the inn's owner, a fiftyish woman with an angular body. "Just business, I'm afraid. A client has some matters to settle with relatives nearby."

"Are you a lawyer?"

He masked his irritation at her nosiness. "Yes, ma'am," he lied.

"Oh." She didn't seem pleased to learn this, but then, a lot of people disliked attorneys. Alden wasn't fond of them himself, in fact. They meddled and they complicated things.

"Well," Alden said, "I had a long drive and it's late. Is my room ready?"

Her mouth still pursed with displeasure, the landlady nodded and pulled a key from her pocket. The key was old-fashioned and well worn, with a frayed black ribbon tied in a bow. "Third floor, first door on your left. I take it you can manage your own luggage?"

"Of course." Alden took the key and hoisted his suitcase. He didn't let anyone else lift it lest they notice its unusual weight. The tools of his trade were heavy. After a cordial nod that she failed to return, he started up the stairs. They creaked under his tread, and the dusty portraits on the wall watched him with disdain. On the second-floor landing, the small window framed only darkness. A poorly stuffed and mounted bear hulked in the corner, moth-eaten and with a scattering of tiny dead beetles at its feet.

Alden would have preferred a hotel, a nicely generic Hilton or Sheraton where the employees would have clocked him as nothing more than an anonymous, forgettable businessman. But this old heap of a house was the only lodging for miles, so he had to make do.

His room was dim even with the lamps switched on, and it was cramped with too-large furniture. The mattress on the four-poster bed sagged visibly beneath the chenille bedspread, and the silvering in the mirror over the dresser was streaked, distorting his reflection as if parts of his face were missing. Surprisingly, there was a television—a small black-and-white unit—and when he switched it on, James Arness was getting shot by an outlaw for the umpteenth time. "Amateurs," Alden scoffed as he turned it off.

He carefully hung his suit jacket on a straight-backed chair, set his folded trousers on the seat, and then stripped completely naked. Standing on the threadbare salmon-colored rug and breathing deeply with eyes shut, he began the ritual. He always did this the evening before, and he'd do it again when he awoke three hours before dawn. It was a simple habit but essential for success, picturing each step he would undertake in the morning: Slipping out of the inn without waking anyone. Driving the two miles to the targets' house. Parking far enough away that the sound of the car wouldn't wake anyone. Picking the back lock—assuming the door was locked at all. Finding the master bedroom and placing the muzzle of his pistol against the man's head. Enjoying that thrilling moment when eyes opened, and the man realized what was about to happen. Whispering—

The bathroom door creaked loudly, interrupting him.

"Fucking old houses."

There was a telephone in this room, an ancient model that would make an interesting weapon. He'd have to try that sometime, but not on this job. He decided against calling his employer; you never knew who might be listening in a place like this. Alden would send a wire tomorrow, after the job was complete, giving final instructions about where to send payment. After that he would probably take a few weeks off before accepting the next contract. New Hampshire, or perhaps—

The goddamn door creaked again.

God, Alden hated interruptions. Even worse, though, was the shivery feeling of being watched. The one thing he needed least in his life was to be observed.

Fine. He'd take a shower and complete the ritual afterward. Then early to bed for several hours of good sleep. He'd want to awake well rested.

The bathroom was surprisingly spacious, so vast that the single overhead bulb left deep shadows in the corners. A faint stain marred the white tile in front of the tub, but the room seemed clean otherwise. No frivolous décor, thankfully. Just a toilet with rust stains around the base, a huge clawfoot tub with an add-on showerhead, and a pedestal sink that might have been original to the house. The oval mirror over the sink was in even worse condition than the one above the dresser. When Alden gazed at his reflection, imperfections in the glazing made it look as if a ghostly figure hovered over his right shoulder.

Shuddering, Alden turned to look, but of course there was nothing. The bulb swayed gently even though there was no breeze, and the door hinges groaned. Alden slammed the door shut, closing himself in the bathroom.

Although it was mid-September and the weather held on to the last of the summer heat, the bathroom was chilly. Alden shivered and turned the shower faucet as hot as it would go. He was feeling out of sorts, which was unusual right before a job, and also potentially dangerous. His work required that he remain fully in control of himself. The long drive was likely to blame, and a hot shower and good sleep would make him a new man.

The tub edge was high. He almost slipped while getting in, but he had good balance and managed to maintain his equilibrium. As the water sluiced over him—decent water pressure for such an old place—he remembered successful jobs from the past, a calming technique that often worked when his nerves were too tightly strung. He was good at what he did and in demand by discerning clients who knew he'd be effective and efficient and, above all, discreet. When the clients wanted something a little extra, a few creative twists beyond the absolutely necessary, Alden was willing to comply for a small additional fee. He'd even take Polaroid photos if the client requested them.

He was here, in fact, on what he thought of as a Polaroid Job. He didn't know what kind of grudge his client had against the targets, and he didn't care. It was none of his business.

Alden paused as he scrubbed himself. Mostly he heard the shower, of course, but it seemed as if there was a voice as well. Whispering. He couldn't make out the words.

Perhaps it was another guest at the inn. Sounds carried strangely in old houses. When his targets lived in apartment buildings, Alden always gagged them securely before beginning his work. It wouldn't do to let the neighbors overhear. That had happened once when he'd been young and inexperienced, and he'd had to take care of the neighbors too. He hadn't really minded, except for the increased mess.

When the voice grew momentarily louder, Alden almost caught its meaning, but then it faded again.

A moment later, something tickled at the base of his spine.

Water, of course, forming a rivulet down his skin. But then the shower turned unbearably hot.

"Fuck!"

Scrambling to turn it off, Alden slipped and tumbled over the edge of the tub and onto the hard tile floor in a tangle of soapy limbs, banging his head and knees.

Swearing steadily, he made it to his feet. At that point the tickle hit him again, rapidly intensifying into a searing jolt that migrated up his back and into his head. He fell again, this time onto all fours.

His vision grayed out. He fought to breathe. His gut, his balls, and his muscles turned to ice. He tasted dirt.

And that voice... that goddamned whispery voice... grew louder and louder until it filled his ears, filled his head, filled his world, and even clapping his hands over his ears and keening did nothing to drown it out.

I'm here, it said, quietly but clearly. Then *I'm here. I'm here! I'm Here! I'M HERE!*

Alden plummeted into a dark, featureless abyss where he felt nothing but cold and heard nothing but the exulting voice. He struggled to fight against and escape whatever was happening to him, but the best he could do was stop the fall and then float in nothingness. While terror clawed at him, he strove to remain calm.

That was, in fact, one of the strengths that had suited him to his profession: his ability to stay composed even when under considerable stress.

"Hey!" he bellowed. "Hey!"

Like a ping-pong ball thrown into a bucket of water, he shot toward the surface, flailing his arms and legs for purchase but finding none. He saw a light, however, and zoomed toward it, crashing back into himself with a soul-crushing squelch.

Once again, he could see and hear and feel normally. He stood up and gazed at his warped reflection in the bathroom mirror.

"Handsome guy."

But the voice that spoke from his throat wasn't his.

Alden's hand reached up, although he had not willed it to, and his fingers stroked his cheek, the touch tender like a lover's. Alden couldn't stop the action.

Nor could he do anything when that hand—his own, with the familiar calluses on the finger pads and the small scar across two knuckles—traveled slowly down his neck, over his chest, down his abs and stomach, to his groin. It fondled his cock, which hardened eagerly, a pet responding to its loving master.

"Very nice," said the stranger's voice. It was a man's voice, but while Alden had retained the flat, nasal vowels of his Chicago youth, this man had a southern drawl. Then he sighed with Alden's lungs. "But not tonight's order of business."

Still naked and dripping, Alden's body padded into the bedroom and opened the suitcase that lay on the luggage rack. The man crowed with pleasure when he saw the contents. "Golly, this is better than I'd hoped. It'll be a long sight better'n the last one. Raymond, you got yourself a good one."

Alden's hands tossed gloves onto the bed, along with the fabric for gagging his targets and the metal cuffs to bind their wrists and feet. A length of rope was thrown aside too. For a few moments, the hands stroked the barrel of the pistol while the stranger muttered approvingly, but then the hands set the gun aside as well.

One hand lifted a scalpel; its blade glinted, even in the room's dim light. "He kept these nice and sharp, didn't he? Smart fellow. Dull blade never does anyone any good."

Chuckling, the man—Raymond, apparently—made a shallow diagonal cut across Alden's chest.

It didn't hurt at all, not at first, because both Alden and his body were still in shock. Then the bright sting hit and blood started to trickle down Alden's torso. He knew very well that this wasn't a fatal wound, but it would probably scar.

Stop, Alden tried to say to whomever—or whatever—was occupying him. But Alden couldn't speak, and if Raymond could hear his thoughts, he ignored them.

Raymond made two more light incisions, one on Alden's left bicep and the other low on his belly. That one made Alden want to scream in terror because the blade was only inches from his groin, and if Raymond chose to go farther south....

When Raymond tossed the scalpel onto the bed, Alden wanted to sag in relief. But he couldn't, of course. Imprisoned within himself, he could only watch helplessly as Raymond opened the plastic box that contained a set of hunting knives.

"It's not hunting season, is it?" Raymond sounded amused, his tone almost singsong. "What were you up to, mister?" Whistling a tune by Fats Domino that had been very popular fifteen years earlier, Raymond selected the gut-hook axe and the skinning cleaver. With a handle in each hand, he steered Alden's bleeding body back into the bathroom and stopped in front of the mirror.

"We're gonna take this slow," said Raymond. He rocked the cleaver blade across Alden's neck, but not firmly enough to pierce the skin. "When I died the first time, it was real slow. My bitch of a wife? She poisoned me little by little until I was too sick to do anything but puke my guts out here in this bathroom. She watched me, too, leaning right there in the doorway. Didn't say one damned word about why she did it. I guess for the money, because now this house is hers and she makes a tidy income. Anyway, let me tell you, it wasn't a good way to die. Barfing blood. Shitting blood. Felt like my whole insides were filled with broken glass. Me and you, though, we're gonna have more fun with it."

Raymond gently placed the honed edge of the cleaver atop Alden's left nipple and flicked the handle down, neatly slicing off the tender nubbin of flesh.

Inside himself, Alden howled. Not just at the pain, which was brutal, but also at the realization of what was going to happen to him. Death by a thousand cuts. He'd end up cold and empty on the floor, skin glued to the tile with his own dried blood. Gone from this plane of existence—unmourned, unremembered—and on to whatever awaited him afterward. Maybe he'd end up like Raymond, a ghost stuck in this goddamn old house with nothing to do but possess unwary travelers.

Raymond watched, grinning, as scarlet droplets fell from the cleaver onto the sink. Blood tickled Alden's stomach, arm, and legs and then pitter-patted onto the floor.

This wasn't right. It wasn't Alden's blood that should be flowing—it was the targets. The targets should be groaning through their gags, breath snorting in and out of their noses, pissing themselves with terror while Alden made tiny slice after tiny slice. Their eyes should be comically wide. They should be thrashing helplessly in their tight bonds. They should be emitting a muted wail as they watched their loved ones slowly butchered.

With the cleaver pressed to Alden's remaining nipple, Raymond paused. "Wait. What was that?" He frowned at Alden's reflection; head cocked like a man trying hard to hear something.

Oh God. Alden understood.

He focused his mind, the only part of himself he could still control, and hurled a tidal wave of images at Raymond. Bodies riddled with bullet holes or swaying gently from nooses. Faces purple with anoxia. And the Polaroid Jobs. God, all of the Polaroid Jobs, with desperate, dying moans and humans rendered to little more than slabs of meat.

Alden's finest work.

And Raymond, after a moment of thought, laughed.

Laughed so hard, in fact, that he dropped both knives. They clattered onto the tile and still he laughed, tears leaking from Alden's eyes and joining the flow of salty fluids.

Still chuckling, Raymond swiped the back of Alden's hand across his eyes and grinned into the mirror. "All right, mister. I see your point. Way more fun to be had if I let you live. We're gonna be good buddies. Let's get you cleaned up, all right? Tomorrow we're gonna go for the seventh death."

Whistling, Raymond reached for a towel.

333

Ben Craft

"Can't we just enjoy the fucking moment for once?" Mel asked.

The moment had always been a childish fantasy, something I had invented in my mind. The sound of the shower conjures up the image of us standing in the rain, anxiously waiting for the agent to hand over the keys to our new home.

333 Woodville Street: the permanent renovation project.

While the water heats up, I lock the bathroom door and undress. I push down the lid on the laundry basket, the ends of my red dress draped over the edge like rose petals hanging on for dear life.

Today is our anniversary.

We've been living together for three years. Three years, three months and three days, to be exact. It was supposed to be a special night, but I'll only remember it as the night we had our biggest argument.

"I thought we could move on," Mel said, "but you're too obsessive. And you always focus on the negative."

I step over the side of our large shower bath and let the water splash against my face, coalescing with my tears. The tile wall behind this artificial waterfall is a constant reminder of our neglect. *You always focus on the negative.* Mel would see their favorite color, teal, in the shape of flowers, delicately painted on the white four-by-four tiles; I only see the burgeoning mold, spreading across the wall like the ivy on the side of our house.

I feel a sense of camaraderie with the mold--we're all just thieves, really, stealing from our environment. We mimic the mold growing in our showers. We blend with the grout lines, each day becoming a larger part of someone else's life, slowly eating away at their personal space.

Until that someone destroys us.

They erase us with the agitated strokes of a scrub brush, breaking us into tiny fragments of who we once were, just spores of mold drifting aimlessly in search of a new host. I feel those spores now. They fill the air, split my lips and tickle my trachea. My eyes water, my skin itches. Can it be my overactive imagination, again?

I think about the spores entering my bloodstream, through the open wound on my hand, the laceration a reminder of our argument earlier.

"Stop living in fucking la-la land," Mel said. "Just act like a normal human for once in your life."

I imagine the spores swimming through my body with the current of my blood. This wouldn't be the first time I've thought about cutting open my skin to remove an unwelcome guest. Something deep below the surface, like fossils on a seabed. It's a recurring fantasy, one that's invaded my thoughts for years. That's why I've learned basic survival tactics. Grounding techniques to calm me down when I'm ready to fulminate. They are less intrusive than the methods I used as a teenager.

The three-three-three rule: name three things you see, three things you hear and move three body parts. Simple enough. The order doesn't matter - It's really just about taking inventory of yourself. Take control. I thought I had taken control of my life.

Move three body parts:

I move my fingers around like I'm playing an imaginary piano. I steady myself with my arm and lift my left leg in the air. I spell out my name, drawing each letter in the air with my toes: L-A-N-D-O-N. Finally, I crouch down in the bathtub, feeling the temperature of the water cool as I move farther away from the showerhead.

Name three things you hear:

I stand up and listen to the water splashing against the surface of the cast iron tub. The sound of music. Mel always listens to music while cooking, usually not this loud, but everything seems a bit exaggerated and tragic today. Then there's the sound of tapping, almost to the beat of the music, but off just enough to know it can't be Mel.

Thwack, Thwack, thwack.

The noise sounds closer to me now. Almost as if it's right behind me.

Three things I see:

I see the oval-shaped mirror above the sink, the steamy glass hiding the spots of toothpaste splattered across it. I turn around and look at the small textured-glass window. A small blurry object appears in the bottom-right corner of the frame, barely visible against the darkness of the night. It moves away, hesitantly at first, then strikes the window again.

And again.

The room is foggy, the air is thick and it's difficult to breathe.

The tapping on the window gets louder, more persistent.

The self-help forums say the three-three-three rule is unreliable. Sometimes, in the attempt to ground ourselves, we focus on things that increase our anxiety. What's meant to help us triggers us--like the dark shape that slowly moves up from the bottom of the window frame, standing within arm's reach, protected only by the very breakable double-glazed glass.

The shape of a hand rises in the air and starts to wave at me.

"Mel!" I shout.

The body of the stranger doesn't move, only the hand.

"Mel!"

I reach behind me and shut off the water, never taking my eyes off the stranger. I try to cover my vulnerable body with each arm, hoping the obscure glass will discourage the creep.

"Mel!"

But there's no response.

The stranger is still waving at me. Waving? They are beckoning me to them. My name is a ghostly echo, cutting through the misty air.

The music in the kitchen stops for a brief moment.

A sea of red fills my eyes. Blood mixing with mold. Carmine with emerald on a paint palette.

The silence is replaced by the pounding, opening notes of '*London Calling*'. Mel's favorite, it's on every playlist they've ever shared. Mel's voice should come at any moment, singing along, out-of-tune. At least that's how it used to be. Back when things were better between us, back when we could speak to each other. We used to cook together, singing along to our favorite songs, both the worst karaoke singers in our own personal bar.

Except I don't hear Mel's voice.

I hear the voice of the stranger, singing along to the song. The brittle, thin voice of the stranger ends each line with a cough. Or is it a cruel laugh?

I can hear them moving towards the bathroom, closer with each word of the song. The driving bass notes sound like a battering ram against the door.

I pull open the shower curtain and try to hop out and around it, but my left foot slips backwards. I fall forward and catch the sink with my hand, but my knee slams into the edge of the tub. Bone against cast iron. My leg feels limp and useless when my foot reaches the ceramic floor. I crawl along the cold floor and lock the door before the stranger can invade my safe room.

Knock, knock.

"What do you want?!" I'm crouched on all fours, looking up at the door like a dog waiting for its owner to come home.

The stranger is still singing along to the song, mimicking my voice now, mocking me, laughing at me.

"Fuck you," I say.

Knock, knock, knock.

My heart rate increases. The room around me feels more and more like a tomb. Muffled voices, possibly, but everything is out of focus.

STOP, Landon.

I need to be present, remain in the moment.

My eyes land on the waterproof Bluetooth speaker, resting on the toilet tank, a gift from Mel when we bought this junkyard of a house.

Three-three-three rule, bring me back down to earth.

Take inventory, Landon, take control.

My arms and fingers work. I can feel the pain in my knee, like the bone is tearing through my fucking skin at this point.

The Clash still blares from the small overburdened speaker, the pulsating rhythm attacks my brain. "Leave me alone," I shout, hearing another round of knocks on the door. Then, I can hear myself start to cry; softly, a barely audible whimper.

I wipe away the tears and see the tiny streaks of water on my hand. The shadowy figure, the stranger, is still in the window frame, still waving; now faster with both hands. There's something else, though, something shiny moving around in my peripheral vision. I look up to see the door handle moving: up, down, up, down.

I shift my body so my back is against the door. My mind sees the image of a knife piercing the wood, sliding into my back, paralyzing me.

"Go away!"

Tap, tap, tap.

I fling the bathroom rug at the window in desperation.

Thump, thump, thump!

The pounding escalates on both the door and the window: the only two ways to escape with my blood still flowing. This room is a tomb, the bathtub is my casket. But only if I let it be. I will get out. I can get away from this cell--on my own terms.

Three-three-three, bring me back to life.

The pain in my knee almost sends me back to the floor, but I feel the sink, cold and wet as I pull myself up. My head turns towards the window, towards the stranger still lurking outside.

Knock, knock, knock – I hear against the door.

Tap, tap, tap – coming from the window.

I keep moving forward and reach for the tap in the bathtub. The sound and sight of the water is almost calming.

The doorknob is moving: up, down, up, down.

The water is hot, but the surface of the tub sends chills down my naked back. I ease into my death box. I focus on the ceiling, my breathing, controlling my thoughts. I focus on the body across from me, seated in an upright position. The water slowly rises around me, my legs parting the Red Sea.

Three-three-three.

My mind flashes to Mel in the bedroom, blow-drying their short auburn hair, frowning at me in the reflection of the dressing table mirror.

Mel is in the bathtub, a beer resting on the edge of the tub, smiling at their phone screen, laughing at someone else's clever jokes.

Mel is singing "London Calling" to a crowd of drunken strangers, but their eyes are locked on me, making the easy and most obvious choice: swapping *London* with *Landon*. It's embarrassing.

Mel is telling me I'm a mess, that I've fucked everything up. I hear them calling my name, shouting in fear. I hear the sound of their skin parting against the blade of the knife.

Mel's hand is on my chest holding me back. They're gripping my wrist with all their strength. They push the blade down and it slices through my hand.

Three-three-three.

The angel's number.

I see myself, strong and confident, dragging Mel's body down the hall towards the bathroom. There's a knife in my hand, shimmering and dripping with blood. I see the wounds, vibrant red: three slashes across Mel's chest, three across their abdomen, and three across their left wrist. I've opened a portal to another world, a world I had only dreamed about.

I hear the sounds of those laughing at me and mocking me drifting away. I hear a beat, steady and strong, my heart beneath the rising water.

I hear voices, louder and louder, breaking through the door.

I move forward, water splashing over the edges, and rest my head on Mel's lifeless body. It's just me and Mel, together again, unstoppable forces.

The door bursts open, cold air rushes into the steam-filled bathroom. The lid on my self-imposed coffin lifts to reveal the flat-white ceiling. I peer over the edge of the tub and see the two dark-clothed strangers rushing into the room.

"Mel!" The voice sounds like that of my mother.

I feel two cold hands gently touch my naked back, lifting me up. I feel the stranger drape my soft teal-colored robe over my shoulders.

I feel the breath fill my lungs.

I close my eyes and enjoy the moment.

One Bug

Alex Azar

Day 1:

I don't know why females get so upset when they learn I'm texting from the bathroom, they act like they never shit. Anyway, who's got something nice on Snapchat? Before Andy can open the app on his phone, something catches his eye near the bathroom door. Staring, his mind is as blank as he is motionless. Then... *Is that a fly? What the hell?*

Andy's pristine white bathroom is reflective of the rest of his immaculately cleaned house. No one would call him a germaphobe, but his friends would unilaterally describe Andy as anal retentive. *Come a little closer, come on.* He rolls up a science magazine slowly, keeping his eyes on the fly as it darts around the small, tiled washroom.

Biding his time, he momentarily forgets about his bowels and tracks the fly, waiting for it to get close enough, when... *Wham!* Andy slams the makeshift weapon atop the sink, exploding the fly in a burst of ash. *What the hell kind of fly is that?*

Pausing a moment to contemplate his question, Andy then remembers his original reason for being in that particular room.

Day 2:

It just feels wrong that LA has a football team. I mean, it just doesn't even sound right. There's a reason both teams left in the nineties. Why would they... "Seriously?" The sight of a fly in the bathroom once again catches Andy's eye. It flies behind the shower curtain, hiding, obscured by the white cloth with the black silhouette of a barren tree. *Come out, come out wherever you are.*

The sing-song cadence of his thoughts contradict the fury in his heart. He grabs the same magazine, with remnants of another fly near the top right corner of the back cover. His mind's gone blank with anger and bewilderment at the bug brazen enough to infiltrate his private sanctum. Suddenly the fly appears from the side of the shower near Andy sitting on his throne. *Hiya!* With a swiftness that surprises even himself, Andy smashes the insect intruder, leaving a smear of ashes against the tiled wall. *Ridiculous.* He can now resume his previous mission.

Day 16:

I know better than to eat Thai so late in the night, but God that was so worth it. As predictable as Andy's bathroom schedule, the same has become true for his nightly visit by the aerial nuisance.

Although he's sitting on the toilet with his jeans comfortably resting at his knees, Andy refuses to use the facilities until he massacres the intruder, he knows is waiting for him. *Oh where, oh where can my fly be?* As if on cue, his attention is drawn to the window to his left. It is set high enough that if he were to stand up nude, his indecency would remain hidden, however the window is low enough to prevent anyone outside a view over the white shower curtain.

Already in his hand, he readies the ash-stained science magazine. It rolls comfortably, doing most of the work on its own, like a well-oiled derby cart going downhill. *Yahtzee!* a poof of ash is smeared on the window, and Andy's tense body relaxes, allowing him to do his business.

Day 19:

Whamm!

Day 21:

Hulk smash!

Day 27:

Popcorn!

Day 32:

"Yea, I'm fine. I'll be out in minute." Andy shouts with sweat beading his face as he waits on the toilet. His friends are over to watch the football game, but he can't think about that right now. His eyes are laser focused, scanning the lavatory. *Come on you piece of shit, I know you're here. Show your ashy ass.* Nothing.

His feet have gone numb, his thighs bloodless white, but still he waits with makeshift weapon in hand. *Where the hell have you been coming from?* Still scanning, his eyes fall to the bottom of his shower curtain. The bleach white cloth has a small gray stain of ash from the previous night's massacre.

Before the thought of cleaning the curtain can fully form in his mind, "HA!" *Did I say that out loud?* He creates another gray stain, this time on the wall just above the toilet paper roll. The joy of felling his foe eases Andy into releasing everything with little difficulty.

Day 65:

Anytime you son of a bitch. Come on, hurry up! Andy has been waiting to find a bug for what feels like hours, but he dare not avert his eyes from their vigilance of the small tiled room to check his phone.

Was that... he focuses to his right where the towel is hung next to the sink. *Is that where you are? You think I won't get up with my pants around my ankles?* Proving the insect wrong, He shuffles two steps from the toilet to the other side of the sink and stands in front of the towel rack. One hand holds the rolled science magazine in a halfcocked position, while the other holds his bubbling stomach.

Whamm! "Haha." *When will you learn? You're my bitch!* Andy's gloats are cut off by his need to defecate.

Day 88:

I can't hold it any longer. Penguin-walking from the door where he thought he saw an ash fly, Andy makes his way back to the toilet, when... *Are you there?*

He throws the shower curtain open, blindly swinging his trusted weapon and slamming it against the shower wall between the water controls and the showerhead. The gray magazine leaves a long smear of ash, but Andy knows there was no fly part of that mess. *Damn it.* "Damn it."

The white bathroom tiles have seen better days, just three months ago in fact. They now almost all have an ever-growing layer of gray ash. The same can be said for the sink, towel rack, window, curta... "Hahaha, got you, you son of a bitch!" Another small pile of ash added to the windowsill.

Day 132:

Where are you?

Day 133:

Where the hell are you?

Day 134:

"Where the fuck are you, you piece of sh...trash?" After days of unsuccessfully finding an ash fly, Andy can't bring himself to even say the word of the act he hasn't been able to do.

"Just come out, let me kill you, and I can go to the bathroom. I promise I won't kill you tomorrow. Okay?" His bargain falls on deaf ears, and he waits more.

Day 135:

"Is this where you're hiding?" Andy rips off the lid of the toilet tank, nothing. The gray ash disturbed by the violent jerking dances in the air.

Andy swings errantly at the cascading gray snowflakes, knowing they aren't actually living flies. "Ahhh!"

Day 136:

Now fully naked, Andy has not only removed his clothes and the lid to the toilet, but also ripped off the doors to the bathroom cabinet below the sink, towel rack, curtain rod, and toilet paper holder. Ash has settled on every visible surface, including the unused toilet, but for five days none of it has been from a new kill.

"Please, just let me kill you. That's how this works. Please."

The only noise in response to his whispered plea is the grumbling of his stomach, in desperate need of release. "I know." Andy answers his own body, with tears rolling down his cheeks. "I know, but I can't go yet. Just a little longer, okay? I tried to go an hour ago, and it wouldn't work." That hour was three days ago. "Just don't think about it, while I kill this fly again, okay?"

Day 137:

Andy has given up on finding the fly. Andy's given up on going to the bathroom. Andy's given up.

Day 138:

Curled into a ball, Andy cries on the floor of his destroyed bathroom.

Day 198:

With much effort the officer was able to break the bathroom door in and push it past the rubble of broken tiles on the floor.

Justin, one of Andy's football friends, isn't sure what he notices first, the smell wafting from the bathroom past the officer or the sound of his friend. "I'll just be a minute longer."

"Oh my god." He whispers as he surveys the wreckage of both the bathroom and of his friend. "What happened to you?"

Like flies to shit, both are now in the bathroom with Andy. "Just be a minute," he says to no one in particular, still holding out the notion that he must kill the fly again.

The officer bends to a knee, waving his hands violently in the air, shoeing away the swarm hovering around Andy. "Sir, I'm going to have to ask you to wait outside." He doesn't turn to see if Justin is still there as he reaches for Andy.

"Just be a minute."

Not sure what to make of the scene, the officer tries to comfort Andy, "It's okay son, we'll get you some help." The smell, still too much for him, causes him to gag. "Why don't we try and get you cleaned up?" He offers for Andy's sake as much as for himself.

"Just a minute."

Day 199:

Andy sits in an all white room, eerily similar to his former bathroom. However, instead of white porcelain tiles, these tiles are padded, and instead of a vanity mirror, there's a two-way mirror. He's also no longer naked, but now dressed in a straight jacket.

"Just a minute."

Day 200:

"Just a minute."

Day 201:

"Just a minute."

The Last Chance

Wil Redd

"Listen to me you little shit," Emmanuel said to a toddler staring down at him from a handicap toilet. He had spent the night passed out on the floor of a bathroom at the Last Chance Café.

"Alright, Tommy, let's leave the man alone," said his father, a portly man in his fifties.

"Daddy, is he dead?" said the toddler.

"Not yet Tommy," said the father, dragging the toddler by the arm out of the handicap stall and the bathroom.

"What the fuck is that supposed to mean?" said Emmanuel, wiping grime off his left cheek. The floor had a thick layer of muck that in some spots made it seem like it had an ugly shaggy carpet above tacky baby blue tile. He struggled to stand up and had to use the recently pissed-on toilet for support.

Once he got up, he slammed the door wide open and saw his reflection in the mirror. The gruesome reflection didn't line up with how he felt. His tight-fitting polo shirt was soaked in blood and chunks of flesh. He touched his face, trying to feel for the exposed cheekbone he saw on the mirror. Then he moved his hand to the gaping wound on the right side of his clavicle. The bone protruded from his body like a piece of splintered wood. He didn't feel any of it.

"Is he one of them?" a voice outside the bathroom mumbled.

"I don't know. He talked," said another voice, of a woman, coming from the door of the bathroom.

"Can they talk?"

"Do we even know what's happening?" said a voice that didn't bother to lower the volume.

"Haven't you seen the news?" said another voice, this one with a slight hushed tone that also communicated. "Lower your voices so he can't hear us."

Manny didn't have time to contemplate his battered body in the mirror. He surmised that a hospital visit was in his near future. When he started to walk, he noticed another injury. His left knee was exposed, with deep bite marks. He felt none of it. When he got to the door, he tried to push it open, but it was locked. He banged on it a few times and jiggled the handle.

"Hey! Let me out, I need some fucking help," he screamed putting his face as close as he could to the door.

"What are we going to do?" said a voice so low, Manny only got the last part of it.

"We already called," said another voice, trying to be even lower than the previous one.

"I can hear you! Get me out of here," said Manny, banging on the door and kicking it with his right foot.

"Excuse me, please, can you be quiet? Help is on the way," said a woman's voice, loud enough that he was sure she had pressed her face on the door to speak.

"Yeah, I need help. I look rough, but I don't feel any of it. I'm guessing that's not a great sign," he said trying to press together the sides of his shoulder gash. "Let me wait for help out there, this bathroom is gross."

"No, you're of the devil now. There's nothing we could do to help you, and there's a lot you could do to harm us or to damn us," said the same woman getting further away after each word.

"Psst, lady, don't go. I got something to tell you, "He said, only pretending to wait for her response. "Fuck you. Eat shit, Christian Karen."

"In the name of the father, the son, and the holy ghost..." said the woman, mumbling too low for him to hear the rest.

Manny tried to recall what happened the previous night. Last thing he remembered was coming to the Last Chance Café because it was the only place open for miles. He was stationed in a secret military base in the middle of nowhere. That's when something important popped into his head; he didn't come alone.

"Hey, anyone, go get Raul and Ernesto. They would vouch for me. I'm seriously hurt, so even if I wanted to, I couldn't do much," he said, turning away from the door and resting his back on it.

When his back touched the door, he heard something move inside him. He still couldn't feel a thing, but now he could hear strange noises. He couldn't quite pinpoint what it was, but it sounded like something was squirming underneath his skin.

"Help is on the way," said a man, jiggling the doorknob to make sure it was secure.

"You can help me now," said Manny, dragging his voice like a petulant teenager.

"Did you say you didn't come alone?" said the same man, still holding on to the doorknob.

"I sure didn't, but they're obviously not there with you," said Manny, finally feeling something, a cramp on his lower belly.

"What if they're on the loose here?" whispered the man to the group outside.

"I can still hear you! What the hell is going on? Why are you doing this?" said Manny, using his hand to press against the area of the cramp.

"He can't be one of them. He's talking," said another woman, still attempting to speak low enough for Manny not to hear them.

"Didn't you see his wounds? There's no way-" said the man at the door.

"-Yeah, listen to her. I'm not one of whatever them is. I'm just a man that made some poor decisions last night," said Manny, now pressing harder under his belly until he felt something move.

"A zombie, a demon, maybe even a vampire. We don't know, nobody knows. It's just all over the news. We thought that's just some city folk problem, but you brought it to us," said another woman.

That made Manny jump to his feet. He went to the mirror and examined himself again. He touched his wounds, his face, his belly, his exposed knee, but he didn't feel any pain. However, he still felt something slithering inside him like a worm. The thought of having a worm inside him made him gag and puke blood on the sink.

"C'mon. What the fuck is going on?" he screamed, wiping bile and blood off his face.

A commotion outside startled him, and he hid back inside the handicap stall. There was a lot of yelling, then a hail of bullets followed by boots loudly making their way across the bar to the bathroom door. He heard a drilling sound, and then something metal fell on the ground inside the bathroom. After a few seconds the metal cylinder opened into a small ball made of speakers. It beeped three times, and then a loud piercing ring engulfed the bathroom. The sound was so loud it shattered the mirrors and lights.

Whatever was inside him reacted to the ring. He felt it divide into millions of pieces that were making their way to every part of his body. When each small piece reached it's destination, it would pop out of the skin leaving an open cut. Then it would liquify over the skin, and solidify into a layer of scales that covered every inch of the body. Manny didn't feel the pain, but he felt the encroaching parasite making its way to the brain. He tried to push it back down, but it was too late.

He was covered completely in black scales, and his head didn't have eyes, nose, mouth, or even ears. When the ringing stopped, a pair of eyes hidden under the scale opened and scanned the room. He still didn't have a mouth, nose or ears, just the translucent eyes that moved independent from each other like a chameleon.

"00042, report," said a man as he opened the bathroom door.

"00042 reporting, host was uncooperative during a moment of temporary euphoria," said the creature that inhabited Manny.

"Disappointing, what is the prognosis?"

"Decomposition imminent, motor functions likely compromised," said 00042.

The leader of the group walked outside of the bathroom and picked up two injured civilians by the hair. They were both still conscious, but with severe head trauma.

"Please, select a new host," he said, holding a short Chinese man, and an old white woman with a rosary. 00042 picked the old lady, and the leader threw the man like a ragdoll outside of the bathroom.

The woman's eyes dilated at the sight of the strange alien creature; the only thing she could do was move her eyes. He grabbed her by the arms, and instantly the scales spread to her. After a minute she was covered, and Manny was back to being human. A rush of pain hit him like lightning. He cried and screamed, while he felt every cut and injury. He felt like he was about to pass out, but the creatures he saw in front of him made him panic and stay awake.

"How?" said Manny, stumbling back into the bathroom stall, falling on the toilet. The creature reached out to grab a military ID and Manny tried to stand up. With a gentle push the creature was able to keep Manny in the toilet.

"Did you really think our species would travel light years to be imprisoned by the likes of you? Your people believed that because we were small you could overpower us, but we were studying your nature and we've seen enough. Your civilization must end," said the creature, walking away from Manny's lifeless body.

About the Authors

A.L. Davidson

A.L. Davidson (she/they) is a queer and disabled writer who specializes in massive space operas and tiny disturbances. She writes stories about ghosts, grief, isolation, space exploration, eco-horror, queerness, and the human condition. They live with their cat Jukebox in Kansas City.

Dan B. Fierce

Dan B. Fierce is a Kansas City, Missouri (United States) native, living with his husband of twenty-plus years and his family. A lover of comedy, horror, and many things in between, Dan has over ten years experience writing and performing stand-up and sketch comedy, as well as fifteen years of writing competitively in online forums as a hobby. He decided to make the leap to become a self-published short story and novel author over four years ago.

Ashley Watson

If you like Ashley's writing, you can find more on her Reddit u/thatreallyshortchick and her subreddit r/ShortTalesWithAsh. You can also find various narrations for her stories if that's your thing. Horror and fantasy are Ashley's go to genres, she hopes you find something in her stories that you enjoy!

Julia C. Lewis

Julia C. Lewis is a book reviewer, editor, and writer. Her work has appeared in anthologies such as Step Into the Light, From the Yonder III, and Slash-Her. She was born and raised in Germany, and also currently lives there after spending some time in the US. Her heart belongs to her husband, two kids, and three dogs. Her favorite book genre is horror with a particular taste in indie horror.

You can find her at:

https://www.juliaclewis.com/
https://www.instagram.com/curiosityboughtthebook/
https://twitter.com/curiositybooked

Wesley Winters

Wesley Winters has been published internationally as a critical writer and a fiction author since 2009 in a variety of mediums. He generally uses pseudonyms in fiction, without a focus on any particular genre, though he tends to spend most of his time in horror and suspense. In early 2024, he will release a collection of terror called Nobody's Savior with Slashic Horror Press, and follow it with several novellas he's been holding onto for the past year. He currently appears in several anthologies, including HorrorScope Volume II and That Old House: The

Bathroom (Part 2).

Kay Hanifen

Kay Hanifen was born on a Friday the 13th and once lived for three months in a haunted castle. So, obviously, she had to become a horror writer. Her work has appeared in over forty anthologies and magazines. When she's not consuming pop culture with the voraciousness of a vampire at a 24-hour blood bank, you can usually find her with her two black cats or at kayhanifenauthor.wordpress.com.

Sheri White

Sheri White's stories have been published in many anthologies, including *Alternate Holidays*, published by B-Cubed Press, *I Cast You Out*, published by CultureCult Press, *666 (Dark Drabbles, Book 11)*, published by Black Hare Press, *Tales from the Crust* (edited by Max Booth III and David James Keaton), *Halldark Holidays* (edited by Gabino Iglesias), and HWA's *Don't Turn Out the Lights* (edited by Jonathan Maberry). Her collection, *Sacrificial Lambs and Others*, was published in 2018.

https://twitter.com/sheriw1965
https://www.facebook.com/sheriw1965

Matthew Hall

Matthew Edward Hall dropped out of university, worked as a fishermen's helper in Nova Scotia, on the oil rigs in Alberta, and farmed in British Columbia, before settling down in Toronto, Ontario.

Nico Bell

Nico Bell is the author of several horror books including Open House and Beyond the Creek. She co-edited Diet Riot: A Fatterpunk Anthology which features fat positive horror. When she isn't writing, she enjoys baking and playing with her dog Egg. Readers can learn more by exploring her website www.nicobellfiction.com or finding her on most socials @nicobellfiction.

Kassidy VanGundy

Always a trend setter, Kassidy VanGundy decided to shave her head in quarantine before it was cool. Since then, her hair has grown exponentially, along with her writing career. Feel free to check out her other work: *Cursed Images: Scary Stories from a Child of the Internet, Cursed Fate,* and its sequel *Wicked Breed* which comes out November of 2023.

Christine LaChance

Christine LaChance has contributed to *Chicken Soup for the Soul, Every Writer,* and *The Alien Buddha.* She is the author of the *L.O.Z.E.R.S.* trilogy (the third and final installment coming this year). She lives in Rhode Island with her black cats, Gaia and Luna. Feel free to summon her on Twitter @TheCLaChance

Hughes Ouimet

Hughes Ouimet is a book hoarder and avid supporter of the Horror Community. This is his very first story to be published. He lives in Ontario, Canada with his wife and two daughters. You can find him on Twitter @hughesouimet.

Jessica Gleason

Hawaiian-Italiian author, Jessica Gleason, is a lover of horror and fantasy in their various shapes and forms and can usually be found penning gory tales deep into the night. She enjoys painting monsters with acrylics and singing a mean hair metal karaoke. Her daytime persona teaches college English and Communications in the midwest. Her recent short novel, "The Fabulous Miss Fortune," just released from The Evil Cookie Publishing in June 2023. For information on her projects, follow her on Instagram (@j.g.writes) where she hosts a monthly horror writer challenge, #WeWriteHorror

Samantha Arthurs

Samantha Arthurs is the author of the Rag & Bone Trilogy, the Dreadful Seasons Series, and My First Exorcism. She is currently an active member of the HWA, and hosts the Appalachian Spooky Hour Podcast. She resides in Appalachia, and is living her best spooky life.

Steven Haupt

Steven Haupt is a fantasy and horror writer and a musician. He is still working on a debut novel, but has been writing novels and short stories for over five years now. Steven lives in rural Michigan with his Girlfriend and their dog Orion. When he isn't writing novels and short stories he is writing lyrics and music for his two bands that play mostly rock and heavy metal music.

Melinda Finholm Morris

Melinda Finholm Morris had a 20-year Air Force career who currently resides in Summerville, South Carolina. She had a plan for her life that was rerouted after her metastatic breast cancer diagnosis. She now creates in writing and visually, coaches and trains through her Start with Self LLC business, and enjoys hanging out with her family, friends, and dogs.

Radar DeBoard

After being born on the flat and barren planes of Wichita, Kansas, Radar DeBoard had nothing but time on his hands. Plenty of time to hone his craft of writing stories that explored the darkest parts of his imagination. Once Radar had received his master's in economics, he took his works to another level, far more gruesome than the last. He can analyze your fear, truly find what keeps you up at night, and then give your greatest nightmares back to you in written form.

Kim Fielding

Kim Fielding is very pleased every time someone calls her eclectic. Winner of the BookLife Prize for Fiction, a Lambda Award finalist and three-time Foreword INDIE finalist, she has migrated back and forth across the western two-thirds of the United States and currently lives in California, where she long ago ran out of bookshelf space. She's a university professor who dreams of being able to travel and write full time. She also dreams of having two daughters who fully appreciate her, a husband who isn't obsessed with football, and a house that cleans itself. Some dreams are more easily obtained than others.

Benjamin Craft

Benjamin Craft was raised in Ohio, providing all the fuel for a great horror story. He now lives in the UK, where he started a weekly writing group at a local arts and community centre. When he's not out dogspotting with his partner, he loves watching films, reading and writing horror stories. 333 is his first published story.

Alex Azar

Alex Azar is an award winning author of color bred, born, and raised in New Jersey. He had aspirations beyond his humble beginnings, Alex was going to be a superhero. Then one tragic day, tragedy tragically struck. He remembered he wasn't an orphan and by law would only be able to become a sidekick. Circumstances preventing him from achieving his dream, Alex's mind fractured and he now spends his nights fabricating truths about the darkest horrors that plague the recesses of his twisted mind and black heart. His days are filled being the dutiful sidekick the law requires him to be, until he can one day be the hero the world (at least New Jersey) needs. Alex can be found on Facebook, Instagram, and Twitter @azarrising or reached by email at azarrising@hotmail.com. Please go to azarrising.com for more information.

Wil Redd

The odds of Wil Redd-Rodriguez (he/him) being a time traveler are low, but never zero. Born and raised in the land of reggaeton and rum, Puerto Rico, but living in the land of Dunkin' and clam chowder, Massachusetts. His human body is less than half a century old and lightly used.

About the Collector

Angel Krause is a horror content creator under the YouTube channel Voices From the Mausoleum. From movies, to video games, special fx, and more, Voices covers anything under the horror umbrella. Angel has stories in a few anthologies and released her debut collection in 2023 *All The Little Voices*. You can find Angel on all social media platforms under Voices From the Mausoleum.

Other Voices Titles

Livestock: Stories From the Un-Herd

That Old House: The Bathroom

All The Little Voices

Misses Claws

Printed in Great Britain
by Amazon

41758439R00088